Julian Symons is primarily remembered as a master of the art of crime writing. However, in his eighty-two years he produced an enormously varied body of work. Social and military history, biography and criticism were all subjects he touched upon with remarkable success, and he held a distinguished reputation in each field.

His novels were consistently highly individual and expertly crafted, raising him above other crime writers of his day. It is for this that he was awarded various prizes, and, in 1982, named as Grand Master of the Mystery Writers of America – an honour accorded to only three other English writers before him: Graham Greene, Eric Ambler and Daphne du Maurier. He succeeded Agatha Christie as the president of Britain's Detection Club, a position he held from 1976 to 1985, and in 1990 he was awarded the Cartier Diamond Dagger from the British Crime Writers' Association for his lifetime's achievement in crime fiction.

Symons died in 1994.

BY THE SAME AUTHOR
ALL PUBLISHED BY HOUSE OF STRATUS

Crime/Suspense

The 31st of February
The Belting Inheritance
Bland Beginnings
The Broken Penny
The Colour of Murder
The End of Solomon Grundy
The Gigantic Shadow
The Immaterial Murder Case
The Killing of Francie Lake
A Man Called Jones
The Man Who Killed Himself
The Man Who Lost His Wife
The Man Whose Dreams Came True
The Paper Chase
The Players and the Game
The Plot Against Roger Rider
The Progress of a Crime
A Three-Pipe Problem

History/Criticism

Buller's Campaign
The Tell-Tale Heart: The Life and Works of Edgar Allen Poe
England's Pride
The General Strike
Horatio Bottomley
The Thirties
Thomas Carlyle

The Narrowing Circle

Julian Symons

HOUSE OF
STRATUS

First published in 1954

This edition published in 2001 by House of Stratus, an imprint of House of Stratus Ltd, Thirsk Industrial Park, York Road, Thirsk, North Yorkshire, YO7 3BX, UK.
Also at: House of Stratus Inc., 2 Neptune Road, Poughkeepsie, NY 12601, USA.

www.houseofstratus.com

Typeset, printed and bound by House of Stratus.

A catalogue record for this book is available from the British Library and the Library of Congress.

ISBN 1-84232-917-0

INTRODUCTION

The French call a typewriter *une machine á ècrire*. It is a description that could well be applied to Julian Symons, except the writing he produced had nothing about it smelling of the mechanical. The greater part of his life was devoted to putting pen to paper. Appearing in 1938, his first book was a volume of poetry, *Confusions About X*. In 1996, after his death, there came his final crime novel, *A Sort of Virtue* (written even though he knew he was under sentence from an inoperable cancer) beautifully embodying the painful come-by lesson that it is possible to achieve at least a degree of good in life.

His crime fiction put him most noticeably into the public eye, but he wrote in many forms: biographies, a memorable piece of autobiography (*Notes from Another Country*), poetry, social history, literary criticism coupled with year-on-year reviewing and two volumes of military history, and one string thread runs through it all. Everywhere there is a hatred of hypocrisy, hatred even when it aroused the delighted fascination with which he chronicled the siren schemes of that notorious jingoist swindler, Horatio Bottomley, both in his biography of the man and fictionally in *The Paper Chase* and *The Killing of Francie Lake*.

That hatred, however, was not a spew but a well-spring. It lay behind what he wrote and gave it force, yet it was always tempered by a need to speak the truth. Whether he was writing about people as fiction or as fact, if he had a low opinion of them he simply told the truth as he saw it, no more and no less.

This adherence to truth fills his novels with images of the mask. Often it is the mask of hypocrisy. When, as in *Death's Darkest Face* or *Something Like a Love Affair*, he chose to use a plot of dazzling legerdemain, the masks of cunning are startlingly ripped away.

The masks he ripped off most effectively were perhaps those which people put on their true faces when sex was in the air or under the exterior. 'Lift the stone, and sex crawls out from under,' says a character in that relentless hunt for truth, *The Progress of a Crime*, a book that achieved the rare feat for a British author, winning Symons the US Edgar Allen Poe Award.

Julian was indeed something of a pioneer in the fifties and sixties bringing into the almost sexless world of the detective story the truths of sexual situations. 'To exclude realism of description and language from the crime novel' he writes in *Critical Occasions*, 'is almost to prevent its practitioners from attempting any serious work.' And then the need to unmask deep-hidden secrecies of every sort was almost as necessary at the end of his crime-writing life as it had been at the beginning. Not for nothing was his last book subtitled *A Political Thriller.*

H R F Keating
London, 2001

Chapter One

That Monday morning began like any other day. Waking, eyes crusted with unsatisfying sleep. A bad taste in the mouth behind the spurious freshness of the foaming toothpaste. A small nick when shaving. It was while I was having difficulty with a collar stud that I remembered that this was not a day like any other, that there was a reason for whistling this morning. I began to whistle. From the kitchen there came a sizzling sound and a smell of toast and bacon. Thinking about what was going to happen I began to feel positively hungry.

Rose called out something. I knotted my tie carefully and went into the cubicle we called a dining-room. There was egg and bacon on the table for me. Rose had cooked herself nothing and she was smoking a cigarette, a bad sign at that time of the day.

"You've cut yourself."

"Nothing." I poured coffee and began to eat, my mind playing round the pleasant thing that was going to happen.

She puffed smoke. "Why so cheerful?"

"Don't you remember? Today comes promotion, new job, that vital step out of one wage bracket into another."

"Counting your chickens."

"It's in the bag, Rose. George Pacey told me so. Put it another way, today means a new fur coat, a holiday in Paris this summer, maybe even money in the bank. Isn't that something to cheer about?"

"Willie Strayte didn't seem too much worried last night."

"He's accepted the inevitable." I soaked up the last of the egg with toast and pushed away the plate. I had been eating too fast, as always.

Rose was enveloped now in a cloud of smoke. "Why did you really ask Willie round last night?"

I began to feel irritated. The smell of smoke was neutralising the smell of toast and bacon. "I've told you before. Willie and I have been working together as executive editors. When I step up he's bound to feel sore. He can make things pretty sticky for me or he can help to keep them smooth. Asking him round to dinner seemed a good idea, though the way you behaved didn't help."

"There always has to be a commercial reason for everything." I made no answer to that one. "I'm surprised you even noticed the way I behaved."

"Oh, for God's sake." I got up from the table, picked up my hat and overcoat from the bedroom and called goodbye from the door of the flat.

"Goodbye." She was sitting hunched over the breakfast table with her hair in curlers and the top button of her dressing gown missing. Just before I closed the door she blew a perfect smoke ring. She was good at blowing smoke rings.

Chapter Two

It was a fine spring morning and I was early. I decided to walk to the office. I didn't often walk, because walking more than a quarter of a mile made my leg ache. I had fractured it when I was a child and the bonesetting job had been bungled so that one leg was a couple of inches shorter than the other. A surgical boot had evened things up, but it left me with a slight limp and when I'd walked the length of a street I usually began to think about it.

Today I thought about our eight-year-old marriage instead, and wondered what had gone wrong with it. No children, of course, that was one obvious reason. At first I hadn't wanted them, and then Rose said she was too old, although that was ridiculous. She was only thirty-two now, and lots of women have a first child in their late thirties. But still no children was the obvious reason, too obvious. I shied away from it, and began to consider others.

The simple truth was that you married one person, and three or five or eight years later found yourself living with another. At the time we married Rose had been a typist in the news agency where I was an up and coming reporter. She was very pretty, fresh looking, laughed a lot at my jokes, always seemed interested in what I was doing. That was the girl I had contracted to marry, and she no longer existed. Instead a stranger looked at me across the breakfast table, hollow-eyed and nervous, a woman who lit one cigarette after another, trying to dissipate in a smoke cloud her fear of approaching middle age. She was right to be worried, for although she could still look decorative in the evening it was now a kind of hard gloss put on at the dressing table.

All right, I told myself, that's enough about Rose, what about yourself? If she's changed that much, you must have changed a bit too. I stopped and looked in a shop window, and the result was pretty satisfactory. A bit paunchy perhaps, but then you might say that the paunchiness made me look imposing, distinctive. A good fresh face and a fine head of hair. I took off my hat and inspected the head to assure myself that there were no grey hairs in it. Then I clapped on the hat again, thinking that perhaps I looked a little foolish. Age isn't the same for a man as for a woman, I thought profoundly. A man at thirty-seven is still maturing, a woman at thirty-two is overripe. I memorised the phrase as one that might be useful some day. It was also a phrase that made me feel sorry for Rose. Perhaps I neglected her, in fact I knew I had neglected her. I decided to ring her up from the office. A celebration this evening would be in order.

I thought about the cause for celebration, and about Willie Strayte. Three years ago I had come from a job as crime reporter on a provincial paper to join Willie Strayte as crime editor of Gross Enterprises. I got more money, but at first I didn't like the work. That was before I saw that Gross Enterprises was something new, a kind of logical development in modern publishing. We published books in four categories, Romance, Westerns, Crime and Science Fiction. The characters, plot and general style of a book would be decided at an editorial conference. This material would be passed on to staff writers, who talked the story into a tape recorder. An experienced staff writer working at high pressure could average twenty thousand words a day, thus finishing a novel in four days. Anyone who couldn't manage ten thousand words a day was no good to the organisation.

The dictabook, as we called the recording, then came up to an editor who souped it up as necessary. Souping it up meant, in the case of Crime, adding the characteristic flavour – sex and violence for thick-ear books, atmospheric touches to superior Eric Ambler style thrillers, pseudo-authentic background for adventure stories. In the case of Romance it meant mostly putting in details about clothes, often lifted from the fashion magazines – at least that's the way it seemed to me, but I never handled Romance. With Westerns it meant chiefly checking for accuracy, making sure that the writers hadn't got the sheriff using the wrong kind of gun or introduced some Indians in a part of America they never inhabited. Readers of Westerns are very finicky about accuracy, and they have no use at all for sex. Cowboys and sex don't mix, crime and sex do. There's a moral in that somewhere. Finally the books went up to the Section Editor, in the case of Crime, George Pacey, who checked again for errors or risky material, and maybe added a bit here and took out a bit there.

The finished products were cheaply printed and bound at our own works, and published by a dozen different firms, all of them subsidiaries of Gross Enterprises. They sold in big quantities to the lower-class subscription libraries, and in stationers', chemists' and all sorts of other shops which got special terms when they agreed to stock only Gross publications. We'd pretty well driven all other publishers out of these fields, because when you come down to it Romance, Western, Crime and Science Fiction books don't sell in hard-back editions. People borrow them from libraries and buy them as paper-backs from shops. By cornering this market we'd made publication of these books unprofitable for other people. It was good hard modern business. When I'd got used to it I liked it.

What were the books like? Well, we turned out over three hundred a year, and I didn't read a quarter of them, but in the Crime Section we had writers who could turn out a reasonable facsimile of Eric Ambler, Agatha Christie or Mickey Spillane. I don't say they were just the same as the originals, but they were pretty efficient jobs for all that. The authors' names of course were all fictitious, but we developed individual styles for each author so that anybody reading a book with Thorby Larsen's name on the cover knew that there was practically nothing the hero wouldn't do, while readers of George Hendry could feel sure that his stories would be no tougher than those of, say, Hammond Innes.

Recently, however, there had been some new developments in the firm. It was in connection with these that I was making my step up.

Chapter Three

Gross Enterprises occupied a square, ugly office block near Holborn. On the ground floor was Reception, Dispatch and the Research Section. First floor was Crime, second Romance, third Western and fourth Science Fiction. Administration was on the fifth and top floor, and so was Sir Henry Gross' office and flat. I passed old Sir Henry as I went in, teetering uncertainly across the Reception hall to his private lift. *Who's Who* didn't give his age but he must have been in the seventies, although his lined face and generally papery appearance made him look older. Nobody I knew had much contact with him, not even the Section Editors. I hadn't spoken to him more than half a dozen times in the three years I'd been with the firm. I was never quite sure whether he knew who I was. He said good morning to me politely enough. At least he knew I worked there.

I watched the lift doors close behind him and thought how queer it was that Sir Henry, who was a teetotaller, vegetarian and non-smoker, should be at the top of something like Gross Enterprises. It was a fine example of circumstances taking charge of men, for he had started out with cheap Self Help and How to Do It books. Probably the change to what you might call rational publishing had been imperceptible even to Gross himself. Now he might think that he ran the machine, but really the machine ran Sir Henry. No doubt he had paid for his knighthood like an honest man. It had been awarded for "services to publishing", which was one of the best jokes on publishing that I had ever heard.

The wording on my door said *David Nelson, Executive Editor.* I went in and found George Pacey standing at the window. I liked George. He was chunky and cheerful, with a face as rosy as a Cox's Orange Pippin, and it took a lot to get him ruffled.

"Hallo, George. Be with you in a minute." I skimmed through the stuff on my desk, a dictabook for me to listen to and a long memorandum from one of our writers, Mary Speed, about a new style thriller. Nothing urgent. I said to George, "What's on your mind?"

"Nothing special. You all set for the conference this afternoon?"

"All set. This is only general discussion of Project X, isn't it?"

"That's right. Priming you boys with what you know already. The actual voting will take place at the Section Editors' meeting after lunch. The conference comes after that." He grinned. "Don't worry, Dave, it's all fixed. The job's yours."

I felt a warm glow inside. "How will the voting go?"

"Don't know that there'll be any voting after I've said you're the right man for the job. Hepplewhite may suggest Willie Strayte, since he's been here longer than you have."

"And Hep doesn't love me."

He waved that aside. "The voting's secret, but if it comes to a vote Hep's got one vote like anybody else. You'll get mine and Bill Rogers' and Charles Peers' for certain. Might get Bennett's as well, but you won't need it. Three out of five is a majority in my arithmetic."

The warm glow began to spread. "Thanks, George."

"No need. You're the best man for the job, that's all there is to it."

"Willie came round to dinner last night. He seemed pretty chirpy. He may still be expecting the job himself."

"Maybe. If he does he'll be disappointed." George turned and then said casually, with his hand on the doorknob, "By the way, you edited that new Thorby Larsen, didn't you?"

George was always a bit more subtle than you expected. This was what he had come in for. "It's got my name on it."

"I'd forgotten." George grinned. "But I seem to remember that there were a couple of points. Can you spare five minutes?"

I followed him down the passage to his room, which was a bit bigger than mine and had a fitted carpet. It occurred to me that I should be in line for a fitted carpet after this afternoon.

George picked up the typescript from his desk. "So it has got your name on", he said with pretended surprise. " 'Writer Sandy Donovan, Editor David Nelson.' What do you think of this boy Sandy?"

"I'm not sure yet. He's very raw."

"He doesn't seem to have the right touch for Larsen", George murmured. "I can see you've done a lot on it. What was it now? Oh yes, the rough stuff seems to be laid on a bit too thick. Look here."

I read the passage.

> I brought up my right hand with the steel ball on it. There was a sharp and violent crack. That's the jaw, I thought. I swung the steel fist again and felt the nose bone break with the impact. His mouth was suddenly lop-sided. Blood poured out of it, and out of his broken nose. He spat out a couple of teeth and dropped to the floor, groping for the knife. May as well make a job of it, I thought, and I stamped on the hand that was groping towards the knife, grinding my heel round for good measure. He cried out like a stuck pig.

"Yours, isn't it?" said George.

It was mine all right. Sandy had written something about giving the thug the old one-two and felling him like an ox. It had needed stepping up. I had given the hero a steel ball which he fitted on to his wrist, kind of a superior knuckle-duster, and I'd put some action into it. "Yes, it's mine. What's wrong with it?"

"Too strong, and there's too much of it. Too much blood and too many broken bones. There are about a dozen passages like that, apart from those where the women get beaten up. Might make people think our hero, what's his name, Slug Brannigan, is a bit of a thug himself."

"But we agreed to go the limit with Thorby Larsen."

"I know. Just depends where the limit is, that's all. Don't worry, Dave, I'll look after it." He looked down at his desk. "What do you really think about this sort of stuff? Sometimes it worries me."

"I don't get you. People read it, don't they?"

"Yes, people read it."

"Well then."

"I see what you mean. Skip it." He looked up at me now and said, "How's Rose?"

I thought of the way I'd left her, sitting in the smoke cloud, and wondered how she was myself. "She's fine. Why?"

"No reason. She's a nice girl, that's all."

"I think so too." We both laughed and I went back to my room. I thought he was wrong about Thorby Larsen, but there was no dividend in arguing. I listened to the dictabook on my desk, which was a deliberately old-fashioned locked-room style detective story. The market for these still existed, although it had faded badly in the last couple of years. This seemed a fair example of the kind, and I sent it along to the typing pool. If a dictabook was so far below grade as to be not worth editing it was scrapped, and any writer who had three dictabooks scrapped in a year was fired.

Then I read Mary Speed's memorandum. She thought we might have a lot of success with a thriller which combined the usual atmosphere of country house life and middle-class snobbery with a certain genteel sniff of Thorby Larsen style violence. Most readers of this type of book, she said, would welcome something a little less cosy than they were getting, as a change. A he-man hero who was perfectly beastly to his girl friends, in a rather nice way of course, like Rudolph Valentino's sheik, might go down in a big way. There was a lot more, but that was the sense of it.

I asked Mary to come along and see me. She was a small neat dark self-possessed girl who had started in Romance but hadn't been able to write quite swimmily enough for them. Clem Bennett, the Romance Section Editor, had suggested her transfer to Crime, and she had proved one of our most versatile writers. It was said she had a thing about Hep, but I was never convinced of that. In fact, I thought sometimes that she had a thing about me, but that was a thought I'd never tested out.

"About the memo, Mary." I hesitated.

"Yes, Dave."

"It's ingenious, but I don't think it will work. Oil and water don't mix, neither do woman's appeal and thick ear stuff. They're separate markets, and I think we'd be making a mistake in trying to blend them."

"Valentino", she said. "And a lot of other screen actors since. What about them?"

"Valentino was different, romantic Latin type. The screen is different anyway, the whole impact of it. We're selling books, and selling them to a market we know. We'll be wise to stick inside it. Agree?"

She considered. "No, not really."

"Want me to put it up to George for his opinion?"

"No, don't do that. I expect you're right, and it's a silly idea. Let me have it back." Mary knew as well as I did that putting up ideas that got turned down was a sure way of getting nowhere fast, especially if you insisted on pushing them forward against advice.

"It's up to you", I said.

She put out her hand for it, and I gave it to her. "Is it true that congratulations are in order to the new editor of Project X?"

"Wait and see." I smiled at her.

"Is that what the conference is about this afternoon? You know all the crime writers are in on it. We don't usually get called in to conferences."

"I wouldn't know what it's about."

"Stop asking questions, you mean. Congratulations, anyway."

"Thanks, Mary." I did my best to avoid any suggestion of a smirk of satisfaction. I hope I succeeded.

After that I tried to get absorbed in editing a straight mystery story which Netta Shuttleworth, our other woman writer, had done with a background of high life on the Riviera. The background was very inaccurate, which wasn't surprising in view of the fact that Netta had been brought up in the East End and that her knowledge of Riviera life was confined to two days spent last year at Monte Carlo. I tried to concentrate on the corrections, but my mind kept slipping back to the meaning of promotion. It would mean quite a lot more cash, it would put me on a level with George Pacey and the other Section heads – and it would be one in the eye for Willie Strayte. I realised suddenly that this was important to me, that I disliked Willie Strayte as much as Rose seemed to, though I couldn't have given a reason for it.

The thought brought Rose back to my mind, and I rang her up, said I was sorry – though it didn't seem to me I had anything to be sorry for – and suggested a celebration that evening. She said pretty coolly that she'd already arranged to go and see her sister, who lived out at Croydon. I asked if she couldn't put it off and she suggested that I might like to come along too. I've never got along with Rose's sister, as she knew perfectly well, and I said that nothing would bore me more, I'd celebrate on my own. Rose said she hoped I had something to celebrate. When I had rung off I couldn't help contrasting Rose with Mary, and wondering again what had gone wrong with our marriage.

I lunched in the office on sandwiches and a bottle of milk and finished the editorial work on Netta Shuttleworth's book before the conference.

Chapter Four

The conference was held in Hep's office, and it was a pretty formal affair. Our ten Crime writers were there, with the Section heads, Clem Bennett from Romance, Bill Rogers of Westerns and Charles Peers who ran Science Fiction. George Pacey was there of course, and Willie Strayte, and Hepplewhite was running the proceedings.

Hep was Section Co-ordinator, a post which was supposed to be on a level with other Section heads, but there was an office rumour that he had the ear of Sir Henry. The rumour had no basis that I knew of; it was just one of those ideas that are always floating around offices. Hep certainly behaved as if it were true. He was that kind of man. We all sat around, Hep gave a schoolmasterly tap with a ruler on his desk and started talking.

"I expect most of you know something of what I'm going to say", he began. "News gets around, and you all know about Project X in one form or another. Now we've advanced far enough to have a get together and tell those of you who are going to be directly linked with it about our plans for a new magazine. For that's what the new venture is. Gross Enterprises is entering the magazine field."

Hep paused to let this sink in. His manner combined lecture-room superiority with chumminess in a way which always irritated me. "We hope before very long to start magazines covering all our sections, but we're beginning with the Crime

Section and with *Crime Magazine.* That's the name – memorable, punchy, and tells the reader what to expect. At the beginning *Crime Magazine* will be issued monthly, but if it's as successful as we hope we shall turn it into a weekly. Nothing very revolutionary about the idea, you may say, but we believe we've got a new angle. It's the personal element in crime that's going to interest our readers and the personal element is what we're going to give them – in an entirely new way."

Most of this was old stuff to me, and Hep's way of putting it over didn't make it sound any fresher. The writers felt that too, to judge from the amount of fidgeting and foot-scraping going on.

"*Crime Magazine* will present the crimes of the past with the immediacy and actuality of the present", said Hep. I remembered that he came from an advertising agency. "We shall take the outline of a particular case, Thompson and Bywaters for instance, Rouse and the blazing car, Jones and Hulten, the Neville Heath case, and personalise it by showing things as they actually happened. Imagine the Brides in the Bath case told by Smith himself or the Jones and Hulten story told by each of them in turn, the way they fell for each other at first sight, their life together, the hold ups, the brutalities and the murder. There's terrific drama in it and George Pacey believes – and I believe – that we've got a writing team that can bring out the real essence of the drama." Hep brushed up his ginger moustache and added solemnly, "Besides it can be educational, don't forget that. The Jones-Hulten case could be a real text on juvenile delinquency. That's up to you boys and girls."

"This imaginative reconstruction of a famous crime will be the principal monthly feature, but there will be several other new things in the magazine. We can reconstruct a historical crime using the same personal approach – the murder of Sir Thomas Overbury, for instance, or the poisonings carried Out by Madame de Montespan. Then we plan to run two crime cartoon strips every month, one telling a factual story, the other a serial involving a girl called Nellie who's always getting into trouble – "

Somebody laughed. Hep brushed his ginger moustache again, looked angry, and said firmly, " – with the police. That can be educational too. There will be a big readers' correspondence section on important questions of the day, flogging, life in reformatory schools, model prisons, increase of drug taking, capital punishment, that sort of stuff. We may have to soup that up a bit at first with letters of our own, but it ought to be popular. And George has half a dozen other good ideas which the editor will work out with individual writers."

How much can you get away with, I thought? And there was George toning down my Thorby Larsen stuff. I wondered when Hep was going to stop being coy, and make the announcement about the editorship.

Now he was answering questions. Sandy Donovan, freckled, young and innocent, said, "Isn't some of this stuff going to be a bit near the knuckle? I mean, you mentioned Heath, who was the most vicious sort of sadist. If we do an imaginative reconstruction of that case I imagine we shall lose some readers."

Hep's answer came smoothly. "You can always tell a story a different way to make it acceptable. That's part of what we pay crime writers for."

Mary Speed came up with a thoughtful one. I handed it to that girl, she knew exactly the right kind of question to ask and the way to put it. "You talked about telling a story from a personal point of view. It might heighten the tension sometimes to tell it from half a dozen points of view, each in turn, show Heath for example as he was seen by adoring women, business associates, hotel managers and so on."

"Exactly", Hep beamed. "We're only laying down the general line of approach. It's up to you writers to work out the particular techniques appropriate to each case, that's what we want from you. All of you will be working on magazine assignments from time to time in addition to your ordinary work. You should get great help from Research – the Crime Section of the Research department has been enlarged a lot lately – and of course from the editor. *Crime Magazine* will be a separate entity inside the Crime Section, and it will make use of all the existing writers and materials as necessary. After some discussion we decided that that was the best way to handle it. The editor comes from the Crime Section too. We've followed the organisation's usual practice of promoting somebody from inside instead of bringing in an outsider. You all know him and you all like working with him – at least we've had no complaints. The editor of *Crime Magazine* will be Willie Strayte."

I never knew before what was meant by the phrase about feeling as if you'd been hit on the head. I couldn't believe it, I just couldn't believe it. A circular saw seemed to be going round and round somewhere inside me. I thought for a moment that I was going to pass out. Then the circular saw stopped a bit, and I looked at George Pacey. He was staring down at the floor, just between his feet. Someone else was asking Hep a question. Nobody seemed surprised. Why should they be, after all, when Willie Strayte was senior to me? I looked at Willie. His lean face, with the long thin promontory of nose sticking out from it, didn't show anything. I looked at Mary Speed and for the first time found someone who gave me a look back that was sympathetic and understanding.

Somehow I sat through to the end of the conference, and somehow at the end of it I went up and congratulated Willie. He turned his dark eyes on me and said simply, "Thanks, Dave." I will say for him that he showed no particular pleasure or excitement. Nor did he seem to be at all surprised. I was the only one to be surprised.

I limped into George Pacey's room afterwards – my leg had suddenly started to hurt – and said: "Well?"

George grinned as usual, but there was embarrassment behind the grin. "Well, Dave. It didn't work out the way we expected."

"That's a masterpiece of understatement. What happened?"

"What do you think? They picked Willie instead of you."

"But what about your saying I was the right man for the job. What about my being certain to get Bill's vote and Charles Peers' vote?"

"What do you think? It came unstuck, that's all. Don't take it too hard, Dave."

"Don't take it too hard." I swallowed, and controlled myself with difficulty. "How did the voting go?"

George paused, and I got the impression that he genuinely didn't know how to answer me. "The voting was private. And secret. You know that."

"But I got your vote, didn't I?"

He said quietly, "If you think I'd double cross you after what I said this morning you'd better get out of here, Dave."

"I don't think anything of the sort. I'm just trying to work out how it happened, that's all. That's one for me. You're not going to tell me Bill and Charles didn't tell you how they voted."

"I've told you the voting was secret, and that's an end of it."

"Like hell that's an end of it. After what you told me this morning I've got a right to know why I was turned down. Did you discover I had halitosis or dry scalp or something, or did Hep persuade you all that I wasn't man enough for the job?"

"Dave, I can't tell you anything more." He got up and came round the desk. He was almost a head shorter than I was. He looked worried. "Don't take it too hard. I'll arrange to keep you off *Crime Magazine* assignments for the next few weeks so that you don't have to work with Willie if that will help."

"Work *for* Willie, you mean", I said bitterly.

He took no notice. "Better still, take a couple of days off – run down to the sea, forget things. I'll handle your stuff in the meantime."

"You won't tell me anything more about the voting?"

In tones that were no longer quite so patiently friendly he said, "I can't tell you anything more, Dave."

Chapter Five

Nobody came into my room that afternoon, none of the writers rang me for any kind of information. Were they avoiding me, or was that just my impression? I met Mary Speed as I was leaving the office, and we went out for a drink together. She said it must be a quick one, because she had a date that evening. I took her round to the Rubicon Club, an upstairs bar which had the advantage that you could drink there at any time of the day. I ordered two large whiskies and we settled down to talk the standard shop. Usually I enjoyed it, but I didn't feel like talking shop. At last Mary said, "I agree with you, Dave, let's say it out loud. Somebody's given you a raw deal."

I finished my whisky and ordered another. Mary put a hand over her glass. "If you knew how raw it was, you'd say so. George Pacey promised me the job this morning, told me everything was settled. I'd like to know just how it was managed."

She said thoughtfully, "I saw Willie after I had that talk with you this morning. I got the impression he expected to get the job."

"What time was it you saw Willie?" She said just after lunch. "Had the Section Editors' meeting finished then?"

"It hadn't started. I saw George go in to it about ten minutes after I'd been talking to Willie."

"So Willie was expecting to get the job even before the meeting. All that stuff about voting for me – " I didn't finish the sentence.

She looked at me gravely. "You don't like Willie, do you?"

"You couldn't be righter. Secretly, Mary, I never have liked Willie. I've always thought he was a dirty double crossing bastard, so that this only confirms my opinion." I wondered why I should be sounding off like this about Willie, who after all had only got a job to which he was entitled by seniority. But it was true that I never had and never would like Willie Strayte.

"He's attractive."

"Willie?"

"In that kind of way. Thin and dark and intense – bold-looking, you know, as if he'd slap you down as soon as look at you. Lots of women like that." She didn't say whether she liked it herself, and I was prevented from asking her by the fact that Bill Rogers came in the door. Was it my imagination again, or did he hesitate before coming over to us? Anyway, he did come over, and bought us a drink.

Bill Rogers, who was editor of the Western Section, was so phoney it wasn't true. He pretended to have spent ten years in the American West, and it was true that somehow or another he'd soaked up a lot of information about cowboys and Indians, but my guess was that it all came out of books and not out of experience. He had photographs of himself wearing chaps and holding a lasso, but they looked suspiciously as if they'd been taken at a fancy dress dance. Bill claimed to have been a friend of Bret Harte's best friend, to have met Ambrose Bierce out in Mexico, and to have been the best man with a lariat out in Wyoming in his day. He also claimed to be able to shoot the ash off a cigar at fifteen paces, a claim which had never been tested.

Whether he was completely phoney or only half phoney, Bill was a pretty good Section Editor. His personal life was said to be a model of irresponsibility, and he claimed that he had never refused a drink or been refused by a woman.

Now this bottle-nosed pock-faced character rolled across the room with the bow-legged walk that he hadn't got from sitting on a horse, and bought us a drink. Mary Speed downed hers quickly, and said her date was with her husband and she must go. That was another shock to me, or a mild surprise at least. I had always thought of Mary as unmarried, and she certainly didn't wear a wedding ring around the office. Something must have showed in my face, because Mary said briskly that her husband was a BBC programme announcer. Then she left.

Bill shook his head at me. "No good, Dave. That little lady's got a sign on her that says *Strictly Private, Trespassers Will Be Prosecuted.* Lights up when you make a pass at her."

"You've tried?"

He rubbed his bottle nose reflectively. "What you don't ask for you don't get. I could tell you a couple of queer yarns."

He could too, but nothing half as queer as what had happened to me that day. "How did it go, Bill?"

"What? You mean the new brain child? It's a crib from the States, but I believe they've got something."

"The editorship. George said it was as good as settled. For me."

"Oh, that." Bill Rogers looked thoughtfully at his whisky and drank it in one gulp. "Rough."

I set up the drinks again. I knew I was talking too much, but this was something I had to know about. "George told me I should get his vote and yours and Charles Peers' – that's if it came to a vote. And it did come to a vote."

Bill grinned, but behind the grin there was something uneasy. "I can only tell you the name on my piece of paper. N-E-L-S-O-N spelling Nelson."

That was straight enough. The trouble was I didn't trust him as I trusted George Pacey. "How about the others?"

"Better ask them. If you want to know." He stopped, and then said abruptly: "Don't let it weigh on you. Willie won't find it any picnic. Hep called a meeting a couple of days ago to talk about sales figures for the last six months. They're all down, from ten to twenty-five per cent. Crime's down nearly twenty."

"Venturesome?" I asked. He nodded. It was a word we didn't mention inside the office. Venturesome Books had been started eighteen months ago by a man named Arthur Lake, who had once been top man in the distribution organization at Gross. Lake began on a shoestring, so it was said, but he'd got into some retail outlets we'd never thought about using, like barber's shops and grocery stores. Presumably he had some money behind him now – anyway he'd got hold of some good writers, built up a fine distribution system, and was rapidly developing into a really serious rival to Gross. I'd guessed that Venturesome was taking away a sizeable slice of our business, but not how much. It shook me.

Bill looked into his whisky glass as if it were a crystal ball and went on talking. "Poor old Hep was pretty cut up. I felt quite sorry for him. Somebody had been rubbing his nose in it, Jack Dimmock maybe or the old man himself. He talked about reducing staff – but it's postponed while we see how *Crime Magazine* works out. Your name wasn't mentioned, Dave, don't get the wrong idea about that. But this is no time to go round with a chip on your shoulder. After all, Willie had seniority."

"I seem to have heard that before. And I'm sick of hearing it. Do you know what I think? I believe Willie Strayte has pulled a fast one on me. I wouldn't put anything past that bastard."

Bill looked both startled and slightly amused. He clapped me on the shoulder and said in his phoney American, "Now partner, you didn't ought to be thinking that way about little Willie."

"Sorry for blowing my top", I said. I wished I felt sure that I could trust Bill Rogers. "I'll bear it in mind about the seniority. Just at the moment it doesn't make things any better. And thanks for your vote. What's that you said?"

"I smell tail." Unceremoniously Bill Rogers got up and rolled over to a girl sitting on a stool at the other end of the bar. "Was that me you were smiling at, or just a passing thought?" I heard him say in an American accent as wrong as a bad penny. He turned and gave me a prodigious wink. What a world, I thought, as I got up and left the Rubicon.

Chapter Six

So this was celebration night. I walked down the street boiling over with purposeless and empty rage. I cursed Rose, I cursed everyone at Gross Enterprises from Sir Henry through the Section Editors and writers right down to the typists. I entered a telephone box, nearly pulled the receiver away from the wall in trying to untwist the cord, and dialled the flat. Of course there was no reply. Rose had gone down to see her sister at Croydon. I slammed the receiver back on the stand and succeeded in breaking a bit off the vulcanite mouthpiece. It made me feel slightly better.

I bought a paper at a street corner, mooned along until I came to New Oxford Street and walked down in the direction of Oxford Street, uncertain whether to have dinner, go to a cinema or get drunk. A sign that said *Gongora Street* set up some sort of reaction in my mind. Gongora Street, Gongora Street... I remembered that Charles Peers had told me about a good new wine bar that had recently been opened in Gongora Street. That decided me. Two minutes later I was inside the Select Wine Bar, which might have been new but was certainly dark and slightly dingy. A rabbit-nosed white-faced bar-man gave me a large glass of sherry and I sat down with the evening paper.

There was no news. The Russian representative at the United Nations had denounced Western warmongering. A Countess had lost ten thousand pounds' worth of jewellery, stolen from her home during a party. Somebody had been carrying out atomic tests on some island or other, and the results were very good. Dior and Fath were showing their spring fashions. A bank manager had shot his wife and child and then placed the revolver in his own mouth and pressed the trigger. He had left a note saying that it seemed the only thing to do. I could see what he meant.

When I came into the bar there had been nobody in it but an elderly man with a beard who sat muttering in a corner. Now I heard another voice, looked up, and saw a girl standing at the bar smiling at me. It was unusual for me to pick up a girl, but something about the way I was feeling made me ask her to have a drink. She ordered a small port and came over to sit at my table. Close to I saw that she was not a girl but a woman in her twenties with pretty fair hair and a sensitive mouth. Her voice was low and pleasant, but she had a strong Cockney accent.

"My name's Dave Nelson. What's yours?"

"Christy."

"Anna, or are you just one of the minstrels? Skip it", I said as I saw her puzzled look. "I'll just call you Christy. What's your line, Christy?"

"Line?" she said slowly, as though it were a question she had not been expecting.

"Never mind, I don't really want to know, I'd sooner talk about myself anyway. I've got troubles enough of my own without trying to carry yours on my shoulders. What do you say we just drop a little something in these drinks, Christy?" I made the gesture of opening a pinched thumb and forefinger over the sherry and port glasses. "Let's end it all together, don't you agree that's the only thing to do?"

"You are a funny man." She laughed with a gaiety that seemed quite unaffected. She reminded me, I suddenly realised, of Rose – of Rose as she had been a few years ago. I don't know at all why this should have been so, for she was not in the least like Rose to look at, but I had suddenly the feeling that it was Rose sitting across the table from me. It was three or four years since I had sat at a table like this with Rose, talking and laughing, and very likely we should never sit at one together again. I found that tears were in my eyes. I wiped them with a handkerchief; went up to the bar and got another drink. The hands of a rather elegant French clock under glass said five minutes past eight. "Thanks, Jack", I said to the white-faced barman as I got the drinks.

"Jimmy, sir." He looked at me disapprovingly. I could only suppose that he didn't approve of pick-ups being made in a bar called the Select, but I was too well afloat on the sea of memory and drink to worry about that.

"Rose", I said to Christy as I put down the drinks on the table. "You remind me of Rose, that's my wife. I don't know what it is about you, but something."

She smiled vaguely, and I went on talking in the way that you can sometimes talk to complete strangers. I told her all about Rose and myself; and about everything that had happened at the office that day. I can't remember all I said, but the sum of it was I felt pretty sorry for myself and I'd had a very raw deal. She sat and listened and said something occasionally, which was all I wanted. *Fancy that,* she said, and *You don't say so,* and *Gross Enterprises it's a small world after all.* Every now and again I got up and bought another drink. The bar filled up with people. I found the sherry tasting rather acid after the whisky, so I changed to Madeira. Christy went on drinking port.

There were waves of sound rushing in and out of my ears now, so that things sounded first very loud and then almost a whisper. There was a kind of rubber band round my head, so palpable that a couple of times I ran my hand over my forehead to try and take it off. And Christy's face began to waver a bit so that I had to work to keep it in focus. When somebody put on more lights in the dim bar I felt for a moment as if I had been struck sharply over the eyes. In the sharp yellow light I saw more clearly what Christy was like.

That was a shock. At first I had taken her for a girl, then I had realised she was a woman, now I saw that she was much older than I had thought, older than Rose, and that with the exception of her fair hair and her youthful figure there was nothing attractive about her appearance. I took it all in – the face which might be softly sensitive as I had thought but was also white and puffy, the cheap black frock with its little paste ornament in the shape of a boat, the black plastic bag with the initial C on it. I took it all in and thought, *Dave Nelson, you must be out of your mind.* Even so I was not quite prepared for her words when she opened the plastic bag, powdered her nose, snapped the bag shut, leaned over to me and said: "You certainly are a talker, Dave. Would you like to come home now, dear?"

I could have laughed, I should have laughed. Dave Nelson to sit talking to a tart half the evening without recognising her for what she was. But deep down, or perhaps not so very deep at that, I felt more like crying than laughing for I had been talking to Christy as I used to talk to Rose and it seemed to me there was something pathetic about that. And something important too. I knew suddenly that I didn't want to let Christy go, I wanted to go on pretending she was Rose. That was why I said yes to her about going back.

We went out of the Select Wine Bar. In my private world where the rubber band fitted snugly round my head and the noise machine kept on being switched on and off and things appeared either brassy bright or half dark as if they were being shown in an arty photographer's shot, I still managed to notice the time on that French clock under glass. It was a quarter to nine.

Chapter Seven

It was a bright night, the sky full of stars. We walked down Gongora Street a couple of hundred yards, and crossed the road.

"You've hurt your leg", she said.

"It's permanent. My best friends call me Limping Dave."

"You are funny. Here we are." A dim light shone in an open doorway, an opalescent bowl with a name on it glowed outside. The name danced so that I couldn't read it. The band twanged in my head.

"But this is a hotel."

"Yes. Not so loud, it's all right."

"I thought it would be your place."

"Silly, I don't live in this district, but they know me here. Come on."

Inside there was a smell of stale food and of recently washed clothes. Behind a desk a ferret faced little man sat reading a comic paper. " 'Lo Christy", he said. "Number twelve."

"You got a pen?" I fumbled in my pocket. "Never mind." She picked up the pen on the desk and wrote in the register. Then I followed her up the stairs, pursued by the smell of food. Just before I went up the stairs I caught a glimpse of another face as a door opened and shut, straw-coloured hair, a putty blob of nose, something wrong about the eyes.

Then I was in a small room with a big bed in it. There was a wash basin, a chamber pot, a chest of drawers, a wardrobe. The smell of food was in the room. "Shilling for the gas fire", she said. I gave her a shilling and walked over to look at the book lying on the mantelpiece. The type danced bewilderingly for a minute, and then steadied down. I read: *The Holy Bible, Specially Abbreviated and Annotated for the Use of Commercial Travellers.* It seemed to me that I could not believe the evidence of my eyes. I put down the book with a shudder.

Christy was rubbing her hands together. Now she coughed. "Two for me, Dave, and one for the room. Be more if you want to stay the night, but I expect you'll want to get home to that wife of yours."

I took out three pound notes and gave them to her. She put them in her bag, took out a letter in an envelope and handed it to me. "My boy", she said. "There's a snap of him inside with the letter. Goes to boarding school and I don't see much of him of course, my husband's family don't let me, but he writes every now and then. Like to look at it?"

The letter was the kind that small boys always write from school, thanks for the hamper, Bingo and Jock and I ate the sardines and half the cake last night, have to do prep now so will close, Your loving son Jimmy – that kind of thing. The snap showed a cheeky-looking little boy wearing a school cap, with his arm round another boy.

I don't know why it should have been so, but the effect of reading this letter was utterly unnerving to me. I handed back the letter and photograph, dropped to the bed and buried my face in the dirty pink eiderdown. Sobs came out of me like great hiccoughs.

She bent over me, I felt her hand patting my shoulder over and over again, maternally. "Don't cry", she said. "Don't cry. I know what it is, you wanted a kid and that bitch of a wife of yours wouldn't give you one. That Rose", she said savagely.

The hiccoughing sobs grew louder. I pulled her down on the bed with me, her hand stroking my forehead and my hair. The confusion of whisky, sherry and Madeira mingled in my mind with the confusion and defeat of the afternoon, and for all these confusions and defeats I found it somehow possible and necessary to blame Rose. To blame Rose and then to forgive her, as I identified Rose with the hand stroking my hair and my forehead, loosening my tie.

Chapter Eight

When I woke the room was dark. I was fully dressed, with my shoes off and the top button of my shirt undone, covered by the pink eiderdown. I got down from the bed, fumbled my way across the room, turned on the light and stood there a moment blinking. I splashed water over my face, soothing away the salt tears, and decided that apart from a headache, caused by mixing drinks without having anything to eat, I felt all right. The band round my head had gone, the noise machine had stopped working. I remembered Christy and looked in my wallet, but my money was all there. An honest woman, I thought, is God's greatest gift to man. A text above the bed caught my eye. It read: *Be it ever so humble, there's no place like home.*

I walked down the stairs and out of the hotel. There was nobody at the reception desk. The light outside the door said *Gongora Residential Hotel.* Outside in Gongora Street I looked at my watch. It was nearly a quarter past eleven.

I walked down to New Oxford Street, along to Tottenham Court Road, and caught a bus home.

In the bedroom I turned on the light by my bed and undressed quickly. Rose was back, breathing softly and peacefully, but as I turned out the light and got into bed she spoke. "What's the time?" I told her. "Where've you been?"

"Celebrating."

Chapter Nine

That was Monday. I had no presentiment of trouble – of further trouble that is – until I was called in to Hep's office on Tuesday just before midday. The morning began as usual, the crust round the eyes, the bad taste in the mouth. My hand holding the razor was not perfectly steady, but I managed to avoid cutting myself. Dave Nelson, I said as I looked at the healthy face in the glass, you're a sham, a rosy apple rotten at the core. I was glad that my appearance didn't let me down, but I couldn't face a cooked breakfast. Between chewing on a bit of dry toast and swallowing black coffee I told Rose about the editorship.

She didn't seem surprised. "I said you were counting your chickens before they were hatched."

"It was all fixed somehow. That bastard Willie Strayte – "

"I told you – "

"You told me. When I want sympathy I know better than to come home for it."

"Oh, Dave." She made a gesture that seemed both impatient and hurt. I noticed that she hadn't put the top button on her dressing gown yet. "It's just that – I don't know. Why don't you go back to newspaper work?"

"Because this happens to pay better than the newspaper work I was doing." Trying to drive home what I'd missed in the only way she might understand it, I said, "If Willie Strayte hadn't jockeyed me out of the job it would have paid well enough for us to afford a baby."

To my surprise she put her head down on the table and began to cry. Words struggled through the sobs. "You never thought – selfish – could easily have had one five years ago."

"I'm sorry." I began to move round the table towards her.

"Go away", she shrieked. "Go away, I don't want to talk to you."

I did what she told me but I was worried, for Rose's sake and for my own. Dave Nelson, I told myself, this is no way for a man in your position to get a good day's work done.

Curiously enough, though, I had no difficulty in settling down to work. I listened to a couple of dictabooks and noted points for alteration. A country house detective story by Mary Speed came up from the typing pool and I put in some snob appeal passages, though Mary had really made a good job of it herself. It might almost be worth her while, I thought, to start writing stories under her own name and try to get on the list of one of the two or three publishers who still handled crime stories in the old way. It was hard to be sure. In Gross Enterprises there was a secure job with a sizeable monthly pay cheque, but you didn't get anything extra when a story was sold to one of the women's magazines for serialisation, that was all in the contract. It was an attractive idea to go outside and a few of our writers had tried it but none of them had made a fortune. On the whole Mary was probably playing it safe by staying where she was.

Just before midday the telephone rang, and Hep asked me to come along to his room. He was behind his desk looking solemn. A young man sat in a chair opposite him.

Hep was nervous, I could tell that from the way he brushed up his ginger moustache. He half got up and then sat down again. "Dave, there's someone here who would like a word with you – ah – Inspector Crambo of Scotland Yard. Inspector, this is Dave Nelson. Now, I've got some work to attend to. I'll be in the room a couple of doors down the passage if you want me. If you dial two five on that telephone – " Hep had gathered up his things, and was plainly anxious to be gone.

"Thank you, Mr Hepplewhite." I transferred my attention to the other man, who was not much like my idea of a police Inspector. He was a slick-haired brisk bright young-looking man in a neat blue pinstripe suit. He might have been an insurance salesman. Now Hep was out of the door, and with unassuming certainty Inspector Crambo moved behind the desk and offered me a cigarette.

"Sit down, Mr Nelson. I don't mind telling you I feel a bit nervous coming to a place like this – the book factory, some people call you, don't they?" His voice was definitely not out of the top drawer. Ingratiating and trying a bit too hard to be friendly. "People say that police officers don't read crime stories, but don't you believe it. I'm a fan of Thorby Larsen myself, but he's a little too tough for some of my older colleagues. One of them, now, reads every book you publish by – let me see – John Campbell Stevens. Locked room mysteries, aren't they? And very ingenious too, he says. He never manages to solve any of them, anyway. You're on that side of the work here, Hepplewhite tells me, the Crime Section." I said I was. "That must be most interesting. Tell me, how does it work? Thorby Larsen and John Campbell Stevens and the others, are they real people or just names?"

What the devil does the man want, I thought? I explained to him the way the various sections worked, and he listened with every appearance of attention.

"You've really got it all streamlined and thoroughly efficient, haven't you? I do admire efficiency. The writers kill people off, the editors add the trimmings, and what's his name, George Pacey, puts on the final decorations. You're one of these executive editors as you call them, and Strayte is another. Have I got that straight?" He covered his mouth with his hand like a man who has just belched. "What a horrible pun. Don't have to tell you that they call me Dumb Crambo, do I? Now, how do you find that arrangement works? Do you and Strayte hit it off together, or is there a bit of friction between you?"

I suddenly felt that I was not prepared to tolerate this cross-talk any longer. "Look, Inspector, I don't know what you're trying to get at, but you won't gain anything by beating round the bush like this."

He stubbed out his cigarette. His insurance agent kind of artificial pleasantness was quite undisturbed. "Strayte's dead."

"How was he killed?" I don't know what made me use those unfortunate words. You might say he'd got me into a state of nervous tension so that I blurted out the first words I thought of, you might say half a dozen things all of them based on my psychology and my dislike of Willie Strayte, but I knew nothing I could say would impress Inspector Crambo. He was after it at once, like an insurance company assessor who's got his first smell of a dud claim.

"What makes you think he was killed?" he asked pleasantly enough.

Cursing myself; I tried to make the best of it. "Isn't it obvious? Would a police inspector be round here asking me questions if Willie had just dropped dead of heart failure?"

"I see that, but what made you think it wasn't an accident?"

"Same thing. You wouldn't come here putting me through all this rigmarole if it was just an accident."

He smiled ruefully. "You literary chaps are too clever by half for Dumb Crambo. But still I should think it would come more naturally to say 'How did he die' than 'How was he killed'." He tried the two phrases over. "Yes, I could understand it if you'd said 'How did he die', but that other question is too clever for me altogether."

"You got me into a state where I hardly knew what I was saying." I was conscious that my voice had risen. Steady now, Nelson, I told myself; don't let yourself be bamboozled by an insurance salesman. "And then we were talking about killing people off." He nodded pleasantly. "Was he killed?"

"Then there was suicide, you didn't mention that. But I expect you'd say he wasn't the suicidal type, am I right?"

"Was he killed?"

"Oh, he was killed all right. Hit on the head with a big brass candlestick in his flat at Notting Hill Gate. Very clever, the way you guessed it." He gave a wide grin that showed a set of splendid teeth. "We've got off a bit on the wrong foot though, I can see that. You're feeling antagonistic to me. That's bad. 'Never antagonise a man when you're asking him questions', the AC said to me the other day. 'He'll either shut up like a clam or else give you a set of wrong answers.' So let's start over again and forget my silly little bit of mystification, shall we? Never can resist it, you know, that's the trouble with me. Now, I'll tell you what I want to know from you, Mr Nelson. You worked pretty closely with Willie Strayte here, must have done. Tell me whether he was liked, had any enemies, that kind of thing. Anything you can think of, anything at all."

I told him that Willie wasn't liked by everybody, he had too sharp a tongue and was too impatient, but there was nothing I knew of that would provide a motive for murder.

He listened carefully, tearing a piece of paper off Hep's blotter and rolling it into a pellet. "What about you, how did you get along with him?"

This time he had telegraphed his question and I was ready for it. Probably Hep had told him all about *Crime Magazine,* but if he didn't know about it now he was certain to learn.

"We got on well enough, though I wouldn't say we exactly loved each other." I shrugged my shoulders. "After all we were rivals in a way, and what rivals do love each other? And yesterday, as it happened, the rivalry was a bit sharper than usual, because the firm is putting out a new publication called *Crime Magazine.* I was hoping to be appointed editor, but Willie got the job instead. I won't deny I felt sore about it, with Willie and with everyone else." I gave him a quick flash of teeth in a smile, to which he just as quickly responded. I decided not to do it again, his teeth looked so much whiter and stronger than mine. "But between feeling sore and committing murder there's all the difference in the world, as I don't need to tell *you.*" Somehow his manner encouraged this chumminess. I had the feeling that we were now really getting on well together.

"I see what you mean. You feel that we ought to look outside these office relationships, into his private life."

"Frankly, yes. I don't know much about Willie's private life, but I suspect he was a confirmed bachelor." I remembered what Mary Speed had said. "And some women found him attractive."

"Is that so? A case of *cherchez la femme,* eh? That would provide the motive."

"Cherchez la femme", I laughed agreement, quite at ease.

"The fact that your wife was Willie Strayte's mistress, now, what would you think of that for a motive?"

Chapter Ten

I sat absolutely still, gripping the arms of my chair. I don't know what my face showed, but I do know that Crambo was looking at me with the same alert salesman's interest that he'd shown since the beginning of the interview. I must have been holding my breath, because when I began to speak all that happened at first was a vast exhalation. Then I said, "It's impossible."

"A fact, I'm afraid." He was politely regretful. "I had an interview with Mrs Nelson earlier this morning."

"But she didn't even *like* him." I stopped to consider whether Rose had said that she didn't like Willie. She had said she didn't like him in the house, and that she couldn't see why I ever saw him outside the office, but that wasn't quite the same thing. "She didn't like him", I repeated rather lamely.

"She admitted this morning that she had been Strayte's mistress for the past three months. She said that she didn't exactly like him, but that he had a great deal of personal magnetism. I gathered that things weren't too happy at home between you, but she was very loyal and wouldn't say much about that. She said she was certain you knew nothing of her affair with Strayte."

"Nothing at all."

"This has been a shock for you, I'm afraid." Crambo was almost apologetic. "Two or three more questions and I've finished. Did you know your wife saw Strayte last night?"

"No. She told me she was going to see her sister at Croydon."

"So she did, but she went to see Strayte first. She left him at about seven o'clock and went to Croydon then. The other thing is that you might care to let us have a statement of your own movements last night from the time you left here until you got home."

"I needn't say anything." I thought about the evening and said, "I don't want to say anything."

"That's your privilege. I know you think I'm trying to trick you into something or other, but I wouldn't be so foolish." Crambo gave a businesslike laugh and flashed his teeth at me again. I didn't smile back. "I'd look silly, trying to be clever with a chap like you. Don't you make a statement now if you don't want to, Mr Nelson. You think things over. Then if you decide you want to say anything, come back and see me. I'll be here for an hour or two yet. Or come along to the Yard, we'll be happy to see you there." He made it sound a positively social occasion.

Chapter Eleven

They say the effect of shock is always delayed, and certainly I felt nothing but bewilderment when I got back to my room. I sat for a few minutes trying to take in the implications of what had happened, but I couldn't get any further than the fact that Rose had been Willie Strayte's mistress. In one way I still found it impossible to believe that, but in another I knew that it answered a lot of questions about Rose's behaviour in the last few weeks. I came to the conclusion that I had better talk to Rose. I telephoned her, but got no reply.

I sat there then, wondering in a vague kind of way what to do. I couldn't seem to get it into my head that this was a problem which at all vitally concerned me. I don't know how long I sat there before George Pacey came in. His face was as rosy as usual, but he looked worried. He said that he had seen the Inspector and that it was a bad business about Willie. I agreed. He went on talking for a bit, but I didn't much listen. Then he said: "That Inspector's asking a hell of a lot of questions about you, Dave. About your relations with Willie, and so forth. I hope you know all the answers."

"If you mean questions about how I was fiddled out of the editorship of *Crime Magazine*, I told him that myself."

"I see." There was a slight rasping sound as George rubbed his cheek.

"Now that it's all over and done with you might as well tell me how the voting went. Bill Rogers said last night that I got his vote, and I got yours to – " I allowed a slight note of interrogation to enter my voice there, but he didn't rise to it – "so the other three were against me, right?"

"I told you yesterday the voting was secret. Bill Rogers shouldn't have said that." He paused and said uncomfortably, "Have you told the Inspector what you were doing last night, Dave?"

"It's none of your business."

"Fair enough. But I don't like the way this is developing. If you're going to carry on a private war with the police you'd better take leave to do it."

"Is that official?"

"It's what I think, and it makes sense. A thing like this can disrupt the whole organisation. The place is buzzing with it now."

"I'll think about it."

"Do that." His voice was sharp.

As he was going out of the door something occurred to me. "What time was Willie killed, did that Inspector say?"

"Some time in the evening. He didn't mention any time to me. You've shut me up once, Dave, but I'll say it again. It's no use fighting the police, just pissing against the wind. Tell them what you know and get it over."

"I don't know anything."

"Tell 'em that then. But make it sound as if it's true."

Chapter Twelve

At three o'clock that afternoon I dialled Jack Dimmock's number on the house phone and asked if I could come up and talk to him. I spoke to his secretary, and she rang back five minutes later telling me to come up. I took the lift up to the fifth floor where Jack Dimmock lived, along with administration and Sir Henry.

Jack Dimmock was generally accepted to be the brains of Gross Enterprises, and the driving power behind old Sir Henry. He was really as tough as Bill Rogers pretended to be, a hard little man who had been mixed up with a good many shady people if a quarter of what was said about him was true. According to Charles Peers, Dimmock had begun as an agent of the Barcini brothers, who got a seven-year stretch for dope trafficking. A couple of years after that he had certainly been involved in a case where five men were convicted of fraud. I had never looked up the records of the case, but it was said Dimmock had been lucky not to find himself in the dock with them. Since then he had been mixed up with some risky stuff in the City, but then what man who makes big money in the City isn't mixed up with some risky stuff now and then? And it was said that he had used some pretty rough tactics in the early days of Gross Enterprises, that retailers who refused to sign up with us would find their stocks of other publishers' books ruined through some mysterious accident like a tap getting left on or an ink bottle overturning. But all that was long ago, Dimmock's name had never been mentioned in any case that came to Court, and as far as I knew he was perfectly respectable now.

I had met him half a dozen times – I had been given the once-over before being finally engaged, and since then I'd seen him glad-handing at the dances and parties the firm gave every so often – and I had the impression he was fairly friendly to me. It wasn't the accepted thing for someone like me to approach him direct, I ought to have gone through George Pacey, but I wanted to make sure of seeing Dimmock and I reckoned there was no point in proceeding strictly according to protocol. I'd only once been up to his office though, the day they hired me.

In fact that was the only time I'd been on the fifth floor, which will show you how much we were cut off from administration. I was feeling a bit nervous, but when Dimmock's secretary took me into his office he shook my hand warmly enough. He was a little man in his late forties, pretty well a head shorter than me. He had thick dark hair, eyebrows that met in the middle, and a restrained Napoleonic sort of look.

"Sit down, Dave." I sat down. "All right, let's hear about it."

"I'm in trouble."

"I know that, saw the Inspector this morning." He offered me a cigarette, took one himself and said while he was snapping his lighter, "Don't try to cross that boy, Dave. He's smart. Come on then, let's have it."

"Have what?"

"You've got something to tell me, something to ask me. If you haven't you're wasting my time."

I had pretty well decided to tell him everything before I came up, but his manner put the finishing touch. I described my whole evening from the time I left the office to the time I got home. I told him of the shock I'd had when I learned that Rose had been playing round with Willie Strayte. Once I'd begun it was easy to go on, like talking to a father confessor, though Jack Dimmock didn't look much like a priest sitting there with his black eyes staring unwinkingly at me from under the thick brows, every now and then tapping ash into an ashtray that was coloured dark green like everything else in the room except the bits that were black glass. The carpet was green, his desk was green with black glass handles to the drawers, the curtains were green, the door looked like a sheet of black glass, an aquarium light filtered through a green ceiling fitting. The effect was both neat and gaudy.

When I'd finished talking he said: "That the lot? All right. What's your problem?"

Put that way I found it difficult to answer. "It's such a damn thin story, such a silly story. It just doesn't sound right."

"Sure it's a thin story, sure it's silly, but it's the only story you've got. And it's true." He stubbed out his cigarette. "It *is* true, isn't it, not just something you're trying out on the dog before you try it on the Inspector? I wouldn't like that, Dave."

Something about the look on my face must have convinced him. "All right, it's true and it's the only story you've got and it sounds thin and it makes you look a fool and the sooner you tell it to that Inspector the better. Now just tell *me* something that you don't have to tell the Inspector. What made you go on this sudden bender? Strayte's promotion?"

I'd left out that part and I suppose I should have expected the question but I didn't, or not so directly. I stammered out something like a schoolboy and he soon stopped me.

"It was that, then. That's what I thought. Now the election was democratic enough, done by vote of section heads. You've got no quarrel with that?"

"No." I couldn't explain that George Pacey had given me such a build-up that I thought I was sure of the job. "It was just that I hoped to get the job."

"Strayte had seniority." It was three-quarters statement, quarter question.

"Yes. I suppose I just miscalculated."

He lit another cigarette and stared at the green wall opposite as if he were trying to work out a problem. I had a feeling that his mind was not on what he was saying. "Not necessarily. I was surprised myself when Hep told me it was to be Willie Strayte. Don't know that I'd have picked him." He stopped talking, and brought his black-browed stare down to me for an uncomfortable minute. "Mind waiting outside? I want to clear something with Sir Henry."

I went into the office of his red-haired secretary next door, and sat there for five minutes. When I went back Dimmock gave me a tight, small smile.

"All right. Shake hands with yourself."

"What?"

"I said shake hands with yourself. Go on." I shook my left hand with my right. "Good. You've just shaken hands with the new editor of *Crime Magazine*. Checked it with Sir Henry and he agrees. Don't need an election this time, there's no other candidate except you. I'll send a memo down to George Pacey. All right? Or don't you want it?"

"Of course I want it. Just taken my breath away a little, that's all." I said belatedly, "Thanks."

"No need for thanks. Like to have seen you in the job in the first place. Got more ideas than Strayte had, better ideas too. We do keep tags on what happens downstairs, though you might not think so. All right. But that's not the point. Frankly, Dave, you're not the point. The point for the organisation is, what's the best way out of a bad spot? Seen the latest sales figures?" I said no. "We're dropping sales to Venturesome, and Strayte's death isn't going to do us any good. People say it's publicity, but that's boloney. My problem is: what are we going to do about it, what are we going to do about you?"

"George said I ought to take a holiday."

"All right. That's one way of doing it, when anybody's in trouble suspend 'em. I don't like it. I say if you've got faith in a man, show it. If there's trouble, ride it. That's what we're doing here. This scatty story of yours, Dave, I believe it. You're a good crime man and if you were inventing you'd have thought up a better one. I want you to know I believe in you, Dave, the organisation believes in you." The intensity of his gaze was almost frightening. "You're knocked sideways at the moment, with this business and finding out about your wife and all. But you'll snap out of it. Got to, in fact. And fast."

If it had been Hep talking I should have laughed, but when the words came from Jack Dimmock they did something to me. "I'll snap out of it", I said, and meant it.

"That's the boy. You'll find a lot of work to do, straight away. Get buried in it. Do you good. And one more thing. I want you to realise, Dave, that we're stretching things pretty far for you."

"I appreciate that."

"By rights I should have choked you off for not coming to me through George."

"I know."

"All right. I'm not, but that doesn't mean I shan't do it next time. I don't want any crowing over Pacey, any 'I went to him over your head and see what it got me.' Try that and I'll slap you down so hard you won't know what hit you. George is a good man and I won't have him upset."

"I wouldn't do that."

"No, I don't believe you would. Goodbye and good luck, Dave." The grip of his hand was like his personality, fiercely hard and warm.

Chapter Thirteen

It was just on four-thirty when I saw the Inspector again. Since riding down in the lift from Jack Dimmock's office I had discovered that what George said was perfectly true. The whole office was buzzing with the news of Willie Strayte's death and the rumour that I was in some way connected with it. That was natural enough, but I'm bound to say that it took me back a bit. Until you've been given the particular look that I got that afternoon, the look that implies you're an object of curiosity rather than another human being, you can't know how it makes you feel. It's as if you were a dwarf or had two heads and when you're like me, a man who values his personal appearance, being looked at in that way does something to you. Sandy Donovan came into my office for a check-up on some stuff he'd been doing, and gave me this particular don't-let's-embarrass-him stare. I asked him if there was anything wrong with the way I was looking, and he said hurriedly of course not.

"Then don't stare at me as if I had the first signs of leprosy or something. I don't like it."

"I'm sorry. A terrible thing about Mr Strayte." That didn't seem to call for any reply. "Inspector Crambo's been asking us all a lot of questions."

"I hope he got a lot of answers."

"He wanted to know how you got on with Mr Strayte." Sandy blushed. "I said you got on well. I said I thought you ought to have been editor of the magazine, Mr Nelson, and it must have disappointed you when Mr Strayte got the editorship but you took it like a sportsman.

"Make it Dave, Sandy, not Mr Nelson. This is a democratic organisation." He blushed again. If there was one thing that could make things worse than they were, I reflected, it was the idea that I'd been jealous of Willie. "That was nice of you, Sandy. Thanks."

"I want you to know, Mr Nelson – Dave – that if there's ever anything I can do to help, you only have to ask me."

"Fine, Sandy, fine." That seemed to be his exit cue but he stayed for another five minutes telling me how much he loved me and trying not to look as if I were something in a zoo. Then I rang the Inspector and he said he'd see me in half an hour. Just after that a boy named Stephens who worked in Research came in, and asked if I'd seen the Kline-Ross file. He gave me the same kind of look as Sandy.

"What file? I don't know what you're talking about."

"The Kline-Ross file, sir. Mr Strayte had it."

I was about to say that he'd better go and ask Mr Strayte for it, but managed to check myself. "Who wants it?"

"Miss Richards, sir. It's been out for over a fortnight and nothing is supposed to be kept that long without filling in an A3 form to say what you're using it for." Miss Richards was head of Research, a fussy little woman.

"Why don't you go and look in Mr Strayte's room?"

He said gleefully, "Can't do that. Police have sealed it up. Just thought he might have passed it on to you."

"He didn't." I realised that he had only made this an excuse to come in and have a look at me. "No doubt it's still in there and you'll get it back when the police have gone through things. Tell Miss Richards that." He said he would, and went out.

Soon after that I went in and saw Crambo again. He must have been conducting some pretty tiresome conversations but he looked exactly as he had when I'd seen him before lunch, slick and breezy. I told him I wanted to make a statement about where I had been on the previous evening. He nodded and called in a stenographer.

"What times do you want to cover?"

"Just tell us about the whole evening, from the time you left the office until the time you got home."

I told them the whole thing, beginning with the drinks with Mary Speed and Bill Rogers, going right through the experience with Christy and ending up with getting home and finding Rose in bed. There were just one or two incidentals I didn't mention, like Bill Rogers telling me about our drop in sales, and my asking him which way he'd voted at the election. I didn't see that they could have anything to do with anybody but myself.

Crambo listened to the story without making an interruption of any kind and then told the stenographer to get it typed. "You'll have no objection to signing it?" he said to me. "Helps us to get things straight."

"None at all. Now that you've got this statement tell me what time Strayte died." He sat behind Hep's desk, apparently considering something. "I don't see what objection you can have. I suppose I shall read it in tonight's paper."

"What time was Strayte killed? Remember, you guessed he was killed. Clever, I thought it was, to work that out. Strayte was killed between eight o'clock and half past ten last night. Can't put it any nearer than that. Your wife says she left his flat about seven, got to her sister's at about eight, left there at a quarter past ten. I haven't checked that story, but if it's true she's clear. That will take a worry off your mind, I expect." He said solemnly, "She was worried about you. She's a remarkable little woman, your wife."

I said with intended sarcasm, "Glad you think so."

He nodded. "She says Strayte seemed preoccupied but elated, a bit on tenterhooks as though he were waiting for something to happen. He told her he'd been appointed to the magazine editorship, seems to have taken that rather as a matter of course.

I gather from one or two interviews I've had here that that wasn't your impression. You expected to get the appointment."

"I've told you that already."

"So you have. You were really upset about it, though, from what I hear." Who from, I wondered? Mary Speed, Bill Rogers, George Pacey? "You thought it was a miscarriage of justice, the better man didn't get the job. Felt very sure of it in advance, too."

The better man's got it now, I thought, but didn't say so. "I told you I was sore."

"So you did. Queer thing that Strayte was like you, also seems to have had no doubt he'd get the job, from a few remarks he dropped in advance. Can you explain why he should have thought that?" I shook my head. "Let's get back to last night. Strayte told your wife that he was expecting somebody, so she had a drink and left his flat. Ever been there?"

"A couple of times. For drinks."

"It's on the first floor, as you know, dress shop below it, office above. Just after seven o'clock this morning Strayte's daily woman, who cooks his breakfast and cleans up the flat came in and found him on the floor in his sitting-room. Skull cracked with one of his own brass candlesticks, probably stunned first and then hit again as he lay on the floor. Unpremeditated, obviously."

"How did you know my wife had been to see him last night?"

"Found some letters from her there, went along to see her this morning. What time do you say it was when you left this hotel?"

"Just before a quarter past eleven."

"Nobody saw you leave? You don't know when this woman Christy left?"

"No. I've told you it was a quarter to nine when we left the wine bar. I must have been asleep soon after nine o'clock. Not much of an alibi, is it? But if I'd done it I would have thought myself up a better one."

He gave his brisk salesman's smile. "You go a lot too fast with that talk about having done it. Don't go thinking I'm trying to get a half-nelson on you. Oh dear." He covered his mouth with his hand. "I do beg your pardon. Do you know what's the matter with you? Too much imagination. You've got to use imagination in a job like this, I realise that. Without imagination where would you be? But real police work, you know, it's just slow and sure. Dull, you'd call it. Why, if any of our chaps had to solve these complicated mysteries of yours they just wouldn't know where to begin."

The stenographer brought in my typed statement. I read it through and signed it, feeling as if I were taking out a comprehensive policy on my life. Just as Jack Dimmock had said, it was a relief to have it over. When I'd signed it Crambo turned on his great toothy smile. "I want to say thank you for your co-operation, Mr Nelson. If everybody volunteered a full statement in the way that you've done, it would make our job much easier. And believe me, when you're as dumb as I am things can't be too easy for you."

The door opened and Hep stuck his head inside. He said in confusion, "Oh – sorry, Inspector – didn't know you were still busy."

Crambo switched the smile to him and Hep, delighted, smiled right back. "I'm not. Just packing up here."

"Ah – that's fine, Inspector. What about tomorrow? Will you want to – ah –" Hep's delicacy made it seem that some embarrassing but necessary natural function was involved.

"Shan't want to sit in here tomorrow, no. Finished now. Sorry to have put you to so much trouble, Mr Hepplewhite, very good of you to put yourself out."

"Not a bit of it." Hep glanced from Crambo to me. I could see that he was bursting with curiosity, and so far as I was concerned he could burst. I left him still exchanging Chinese courtesies with the Inspector, and got my hat and coat. On the way out, in the reception hall, I passed Sir Henry and Jack Dimmock, also on their way out. Dimmock said, "Night, Dave", and flicked an eyelid at me in a wink. Sir Henry gave me a thin, wavering smile.

Chapter Fourteen

I felt disinclined to go home, reluctant to see Rose and start myself moving on the merry-go-round of question and answer that was bound to start up as soon as I entered the flat. But habit was stronger than reluctance – habit, curiosity, wounded pride, call it what you like. I wanted to take apart this relationship Rose had had with Willie Strayte, examine every link of it, find out exactly what had made her go to bed with him. Inwardly I knew that taking their relationship apart wouldn't tell me any more about it, but knowing that didn't seem to make any difference.

So I went to the place we called home, which was Flat 14 in a medium size block named Bellamy Court. With a slight sense of drama I turned the key in the lock and opened the front door, but as soon as I stepped into the tiny hall I knew that Rose wasn't there. I didn't really need the confirmatory look in sitting-room, dining-room (table cleared but crumbs still on the cloth), kitchen (plates and dishes from breakfast stacked in the sink) and bedroom. I said aloud: "David Nelson, your wife has walked out on you."

I wandered aimlessly again through the rooms, touching things here and there. I looked in wardrobe and chest of drawers and nodded wisely to myself; saying – again out loud: "Taken enough stuff for a couple of weeks. The walk-out is good and proper, David." Then I saw the note. I should have seen it before since it lay, a blue sheet, in the middle of an almost empty dressing table. The note said, in Rose's hasty flowing hand:

> Dave. Have gone to stay with Marian. Think it best we don't see each other. Rose.

Marian was her sister at Croydon, an interfering bitch. She meant well, people said, which is what they always say about people who do very badly. Rose had always had the habit of going to see Marian when anything went wrong, and for my money Marian was responsible as much as anybody for the trouble we'd had. I felt angry that Rose had gone to cry on Marian's shoulder and indignant that she had left without washing up the breakfast things. "The lazy slut", I said bitterly as I stood there looking at the blue sheet.

I held the paper in a hand that shook slightly, turning it over and over, trying to drag subtleties of meaning out of the few words written there. Then I left the flat, took a bus to Victoria and a train from Victoria to Croydon. If Rose had wanted to make sure I would come after her, she could have found no better way of doing it than by going down to Marian.

I've made it clear that I didn't get on with Marian, and I got on even less with Marian's schoolmaster husband James. He was earnest and she was soulful. He would listen for hours to talks on the Third Programme. Didn't matter what the talks were about – music, modern poetry, the decay of religion, eighteenth-century architecture, anything – the fact that they were on the Third Programme was a guarantee for him that they were the genuine cultural article, and that was what he was after. If you asked him whether he agreed with any of it he would blink his weak eyes behind his glasses, drop his goat's head on one side and say: "Oo-ah – don't know that I exactly *agree,* but it's very interesting don't you think?"

Then Marian would chime in. "It's the modern trend, you know, and James likes to keep up with the modern trend."

Marian wore dirty blouses, shapeless skirts and sandals. She also very often wore wooden earrings, and clattering wooden bracelets on her arms.

James and Marian were great enthusiasts for the ballet, promenade concerts, sunbathing and vegetarianism. They had two children, Evadne aged six and Adrian aged three. They thought my occupation anti-social, whatever that meant, and regarded me with a distrust and dislike which was heartily reciprocated.

I thought about James and Marian on the short journey down in the train, and had worked myself into a satisfactory state of fury by the time I rang the bell of their semi-detached villa residence near East Croydon station. James' mild goat face appeared in the doorway. He blinked at me rapidly, with evident surprise.

"I want to see Rose."

My tone was not meant to be truculent, but James drew back a step. "Oh."

"She left a note to say she was coming here." I waved the blue sheet. "Aren't you going to let me in."

"Sh." James looked round nervously. "Evadne is just going to bed. Yes, you had better come in, though I don't know – " He left the sentence unfinished and led me into a room where van Gogh and Degas prints maintained the atmosphere created by rugs from Heal's and folkweave curtains.

"Marian will be – ah – down in a moment."

"It's not Marian I've come to see. I don't mind if Marian stays upstairs all the evening. I want to see Rose."

"Rose", James said, as if he were hearing the name for the first time. Then he nodded in goatish comprehension. "Oh yes, Rose."

"My wife."

"Quite, quite." James kept near the door and twirled about on one leg. "Here is Marian", he said with evident relief.

Marian was wearing the earrings and the bracelets, and she rattled them as though ready for battle. The corkscrew curls on her head shook. She was obviously not pleased to see me. "I'm surprised that you should come here. Didn't you get Rose's note?"

"I didn't come here to see you. I came to see Rose." I felt that I was behaving with exemplary patience.

"Rose does not wish to see you."

"Then let her tell me so." I strode out to the hall and called loudly, "Rose."

She appeared at the head of the stairs with Evadne who, in spite of her name and her parents, was quite a pleasant little girl. Evadne cried "Uncle David", ran down the stairs and jumped into my arms. James and Marian looked on disapprovingly. I picked Evadne up, lifted her to the ceiling and pretended to drop her. She was no light weight.

"What have you brought me, Uncle David?"

Rose must have been bathing Evadne. She came slowly down the stairs, untying an apron.

I felt in my pockets. "I declare, I've forgotten it."

"What is it?"

"A real princess made of pink sugar with a mauve sugar hat, blue sugar eyes, a red sugar mouth and a pink sugar frock." I had seen the princess in a sweet shop near the office, and it was true that I had meant to buy it for Evadne.

"What can I do with her?"

"Eat her, what do you think?"

"Which part shall I eat first?"

"I should eat the hat first, I think. Those mauve hats have got a rather nice mauvish taste. After that, left arm, left leg, right arm, right leg and then, crunch, crunch, bite her in half."

Evadne nodded. "When will you bring her? Next time. But when will next time be?"

Rose had stopped halfway down the stairs, a curious expression on her face.

Marian dashed forward, beside herself with annoyance, earrings jangling. "Evadne, you are not to pester people asking for things. Come along, time for bed."

"Good night, Uncle David." I kissed Evadne's forehead while Marian put up an arm in scandalised protest. "Don't forget that princess next time."

"I won't."

"Good night Daddy, good night Auntie Rose." At the top of the stairs she turned. "What's her name?"

"Who?"

"The Princess."

"Oh. Evangeline. The pink sugar princess Evangeline."

She went towards her bedroom chanting, "The pink sugar princess Evangeline." Marian followed grimly.

Slowly, step by step, Rose came down the stairs. Perhaps the light was kind to her, but in a simple yellow blouse and dark blue skirt she seemed to me to look more attractive than she had done for years. "I never thought you'd come here."

"Why not? We've got things to talk about."

"Not any more. I've tried to talk to you often enough in the last couple of years and never managed it. Now it's too late."

"Too late." The words had no meaning for me.

"I'm afraid", James bleated from the door of the front sitting-room, "that you don't quite understand the position. Rose has come here for – ah – protection."

I parroted the word. "Protection." Then I grasped what he meant. "Protection, I see. You mean protection from a murderer."

"You said it yourself", said Marian sepulchrally, appearing again suddenly at the head of the stairs.

The whole scene seemed to me absolutely unreal. There was Marian at the head of the stairs, Rose almost at the foot, James at the sitting-room door ready, it occurred to me, to beat a retreat in case of violence. As I looked at their solemn faces the absurdity of the situation was too much for me. I burst out laughing. My laughter did nothing to change the preternatural gravity of the faces staring at me from the head of the stairs or the sitting-room door, but across Rose's face there passed for a moment a faint and timid smile, which was immediately replaced by an expression of doubt.

"Come on", I said to her. "Can't you see I'm not in a murdering mood." I took her hand and she let me lead her down the last two or three stairs. We went back into the front sitting-room, James carefully retreating before us.

Marian followed and spoke harsh words in the accent of extreme suburban refinement that she cultivated. "You can laugh about it, but the fact is that Rose came here today in a state of collapse. Whether it's true or not, she's afraid you had a part in killing that man."

I said softly, "And did she tell you why I might have killed Willie Strayte."

"She said it was because you loved her" (even at this moment I could not avoid noticing the way Marian said *lurved),* "but I told her to get that idea out of her head. Then she said you might have been angry at Strayte's promotion, and thought you'd been tricked. I said that was a possible motive for murder in your case but as for murder because you *lurved* her, that could be ruled out."

"Rose, I want to talk to you alone."

"Don't be weak", said Marian, her corkscrew curls bobbing.

Rose clasped her hands, in a manner that made her look both youthful and defenceless. "You'd better leave us, Marian."

"Are you sure that's wise?"

"For an emancipated woman, Marian", I said, "you're certainly behaving in a thoroughly Victorian way."

That was really a stab in the back because if there is one thing Marian prides herself on it is her emancipation, and *Victorian* is almost the strongest term of abuse in her vocabulary. She flushed, told Rose that she would be next door if she were wanted, and went out followed by James, who seemed glad to get away.

Now that we were left together, what was there to say? All the anger I felt in the train had drained away from me, leaving only an awareness of this woman who was at once my wife and a stranger, and of the room that was like so many other rooms in so many other semi-detached houses, furnished in other people's good taste.

With this feeling of talking to a stranger, with unspoken words like *deceit* and *betrayal* moving inside me, I said, "You don't really believe I had anything to do with Willie?" She did not answer. "I knew nothing about it until that Inspector came into the office this morning. It knocked me sideways. I'd never thought of such a thing. Don't you believe me?"

"I suppose so." Her voice was flat. It was as though she were in a way disappointed. "It was fairly obvious really about Willie and me, I expect that was why I thought it."

"Not to me it wasn't. I thought you disliked him."

She was staring at the electric fire that James had considerately turned on. I could see only the curve of her cheek, a loop of hair hanging loose above it. "Perhaps I did. Liked, disliked, what difference does it make? When you reach my age you want – I don't know what you'd call it – reassurance. I got that from Willie."

"Three months, the Inspector said. You must have needed a lot of reassurance." She did not answer this juvenile sarcasm, did not seem even to notice it. "And I don't need to ask what Willie got from you."

Now she did answer me, in a low voice. "If you could stop thinking about yourself for a minute you'd know that Willie did get something special from going with me."

"He was jealous. I'm a big man, he was a little one. That's true, even though I've got a gammy leg. He had an inferiority complex."

"That's the way you put it. Willie said you were blown up like a balloon with conceit and some day when somebody let the air out you'd shrink to your proper size of a pea."

"Fine faithful wife I have listening to such things."

Again she took no notice of the sarcasm, but went on as if she were thinking aloud. "What I'm trying to say is that Willie hated you and part of the pleasure he got from going with me came from that. I didn't like that, but there was something about him – " She broke off. "I'm trying as hard as I can to be honest with you, Dave. Why don't you try to be honest with me too, instead of thinking about how much you've been hurt?"

I ignored that, as she'd been ignoring my remarks. "What happened last night?"

"What does it matter?"

"I'll tell you." I had thought this out a little too in the train. "That Inspector said Willie knew he was going to get the editorship. Right?"

"He seemed very certain about it, yes. Said it would be part of a deflationary process that would be healthy for you, since you were expecting the job yourself. I tried to warn you, but you wouldn't be told."

"I had my reasons." I told her again about what George Pacey had said to me. She did not seem much interested. "Do you see what it means? The only one certain to vote against me, according to George, was Hep. One of the others, Bennett, might have done – and in fact he must have done since I lost the vote. But George said he and Bill Rogers and Charles Peers were solid for me, so that the election should have been settled. Now, how did I lose it? Why was Willie so certain of election? I'll tell you. Because he knew something about one of those boys that made him vote Willie's way."

"Perhaps."

"And that was only the first turn of the screw. Once Willie had got himself elected he asked for more. Not money, but a better position still. Say it was George Pacey, he might have told

George that he wanted the job of Crime Section head in a few months' time. Say it was Hep and he'd got Hep to fiddle the ballot somehow. Now he tells Hep that he wants the job of co-ordinator. George or Hep or whoever it is makes a date to come along and talk it over with Willie, loses his temper, hits him with this brass candlestick, and there you are. What's wrong with that?"

She turned her face towards me, one side of it delicately flushed by the electric fire.

"It could have happened, I suppose, but it's only an idea. It seems far-fetched. You haven't any proof."

From the next room came the sound of a bleating voice, remarkably like James', but recognisable after a moment as a product of the radio, and almost certainly of the Third Programme. Marian had evidently decided that her little sister was upon this occasion reasonably safe.

I spoke fast. "Don't you see that's why I want to find out what Willie had been saying about this job. Tell me anything you remember, anything."

"There wasn't anything. He simply seemed certain that he would get it. He didn't trust me, you know, that wasn't our relationship at all." She laughed shortly. "He thought I was too faithful to you for that."

"But last night now – there must have been something."

She looked away from me again and spoke in a flat voice. I got to his flat about a quarter to six – that was our usual time when you were going out drinking. He'd given me a key. He came in five minutes afterwards, and we talked. He told me he'd got the editorship, said I should have seen your face, spoke as though it was a foregone conclusion." She hesitated. "Are you sure he wasn't right? Perhaps George Pacey was just telling a story when he said it was coming to you."

"Quite sure, yes." I said it almost angrily.

"Well, then he said that there were going to be big changes in the organization, that sales were down and the whole thing needed a shake-up. He said a bit about you, very condescending, you'd be all right in your job as executive editor, something like that. Something about a boy called Donovan, who was not the right type and would have to go. Soon after that I left. Willie said he had an appointment later on that evening. He seemed excited, pleased about something. It could have been the magazine editorship of course, but it didn't seem like that."

"When he said he had an appointment, weren't you curious? Didn't you try to find out who it was with?" I said bitterly, "After all, it might have been with another woman."

Her voice had an assumption of weary superiority that infuriated me. "You don't understand at all, do you? I didn't care who Willie was seeing or how many women he had."

"And that was all?"

"That was all, yes. We had a drink. I left just before seven o'clock and came down here. There was something I wanted to talk about with Marian."

"What?"

"Never mind. I didn't feel like taking part in your – celebration. I knew there'd be nothing to celebrate."

"It wasn't much of a celebration." I told her about the drinks, but not about Christy and the hotel. I said I'd gone to a cinema and fallen asleep there. Why I should have lied about such a thing after what she had told me about herself, I simply don't know. When I had finished we sat looking at each other. I told myself, this is your chance, Dave Nelson. If you don't get her back now you have to fight it out alone. And in that moment I felt simple terror of fighting it out alone, I felt that the whole world was hostile to me and that I badly needed her help in what was coming.

"It's time we went." She got up with me, and I put my hand on her arm. I swear at that moment she was ready to come with me. Then I thought of something she didn't know. "I've got the job."

"What job?"

"The one Willie Strayte fiddled me out of. I had an interview with Jack Dimmock, he spoke to the old man, and the job's mine. I thought she'd be pleased, but she didn't show any pleasure. "Dimmock said he thought I should have been appointed in the first place. Must be something inside my brain box besides hot air, after all. This is a real step up, Rosie. Let's both forget about Willie and think about a blue-eyed ray of sunshine in the house, one that likes pink sugar princesses." I felt a glow of self-satisfaction as I said it; the kind of glow you feel from doing something beyond the line of duty.

Rose took my hand off her arm. "No."

"What do you mean, no? What's wrong now? You're not still thinking I killed Willie Strayte."

Her face was white but composed. I couldn't help thinking that she looked more than ordinarily pretty, she looked almost beautiful. "I don't know about that. But we can't go on living together, it's no use."

"But why, why? What have I said? God damn it, you'd think if I were willing to forgive and forget – "

"It's no use", she said over and over again. "It's no use."

"Very well." I spoke loudly, maybe even in a shout. "Go and cry on your sister's shoulder. I wish you both joy of each other."

I shut the door. The radio was turned off in the other room and James' head, goatish but frightened, peered round into the passage. "Give my love to the Third Programme", I said, and banged the front door behind me.

Chapter Fifteen

Before I'd been in the office ten minutes next day, Hep called me in. Jack Dimmock had been as good as his word. I was appointed editor of *Crime Magazine* as of that a.m. Hep simply gave me the news and was pretty curt about it. He and I had never been bosom friends.

"Hep", I said to him. "Satisfy my idle curiosity, now that it's all over and doesn't matter. How did the voting go between Willie Strayte and me?"

"Voting?" He had been looking down at his desk. Now he stared at me, brushing up his ginger moustache. "Can't say anything about that. I'm afraid."

And I ought to have known better than to ask you, I thought. I couldn't resist trying just once more. "Your vote went to Willie, I guess."

"I don't see why you should guess anything of the sort. It's no use fishing, I wouldn't tell you anything even if – " He stopped.

"Even if what?"

"Nothing."

Half an hour later George Pacey came in. "Congratulations", he said. He didn't look very congratulatory.

"Thanks, George."

"I'll pass over the stuff that's been worked out on the project so far. It's pretty much uncoordinated, good and bad ideas mixed up. Get the writers on to it as soon as you can. Use anybody you like, we've built up a reserve of ordinary crime stuff." He hesitated. "I hope you know what you're doing, Dave. Willie dies, you take over straight away. It's kind of – I don't know how to put it – people are going to talk."

"Let them talk. Do you think I should have turned it down?"

"Might have been better to let it ride for a few weeks. I could have handled the stuff for that time."

"There are two ways of facing trouble like this. One way is to go on leave – that's what you suggested yesterday – the other way is to ride it. The organization's doing it that way, and I appreciate it." This slight variation on Jack Dimmock's words of wisdom did not seem to impress George greatly.

"It's up to you", he said pacifically. "I'm behind you anyway, you know that."

"Yes, I know that."

They sent me in all the stuff on Project X, which was now to become *Crime Magazine*. It had come in from Willie's room, which was now free of police supervision, and it gave me a queer feeling to look through it and see his writing. As George had said there was nothing very concrete, a collection of bright ideas. The basic line had been laid down, of course, that crime stories were to be made personal. That had been settled well before Hep gave us his talk, and it was a good idea. The trick was going to be avoiding a monotonous similarity of presentation after the first issue or two. There were a lot of other tricks too, like getting the maximum out of all the stories without running into libel or stepping over the line so that they could be called pornographic. Typically Willie had put in a memorandum about the project which was almost solely concerned with these subsidiary problems. It occurred to me that this memorandum was a proof in a way that Willie had felt confident about getting the editorship. It struck me too that I'd felt confident, but hadn't bothered to write a memorandum. That showed one kind of difference between us – Willie was neat, petty and methodical, I was more the inspired type.

I'd reached this point when I had another visitor, in the shape of Miss Richards, head of Research. It wasn't a very good shape, being short and dumpy with a large round head, frizzy hair and rimless spectacles. She gasped out words as though perpetually short of breath, as perhaps she was. "You're taking over this – project X – that Mr Strayte was going to handle." I admitted it. "And you've got all his – papers about it."

"I don't know about all. Some of them certainly."

"Then no doubt you have the – Kline-Ross file – which should have been returned – a week ago."

I glanced through the stuff they'd sent me. All the Crime Research files were a particularly odious shade of salmon pink, and I saw at a glance it wasn't there. I told her so.

Miss Richards' voice became shrill. "It really is too bad – impossible to keep an efficient Research Department – people will *not* fill in the A3 form – would *never* have expected Mr Strayte – " She stopped, abashed no doubt at this slight criticism of the dead.

"Perhaps the police found something interesting about it, and kept it."

"No. I asked them – and they said they had not *seen* it."

I became mildly curious. "I suppose there's no doubt it did go to Mr Strayte."

She waved a salmon pink card. "Three weeks and two days ago." I believed her. To do her justice she ran the Research department pretty well.

"What did he want it for, do you know?" It was very unusual for an executive editor, like Willie or myself to ask for a file direct. The writers were supposed to browse about among the real-life crime stories in the file in their spare time, and when they found something interesting that might be useful for a book they would generally send up a memo about it rather than pass on the file.

"I've no idea."

It occurred to me that it would have been in line with Willie's character to ask for the file personally if there was something in it that might be used for *Crime Magazine* which he could spring on us all later on as a surprise.

"And what was the Kline-Ross case?"

"Really, Mr Nelson." Miss Richards managed to convey that she was slightly offended by the thought that she might be expected to know what was in the files, when her job was only to look after them.

"But you have a note on the cards about the nature of the material, don't you?"

With a gesture of exasperation Miss Richards held out the card. I read:

Kline-Ross case, 1923. Murder Trial.

Court proceedings (newspaper reports). Biogs. of Kline and Ross (special articles). Sentence, imprisonment and escape (newspaper reports).

It didn't tell me much, and it certainly didn't tell me why Willie Strayte had asked for the file. My interest evaporated. I gave back the card to Miss Richards. "Sorry. I'll let you know if I come across it." She snorted. "Don't take it to heart. It'll be all the same in a hundred years."

She left, indicating clearly that she thought my attitude towards important matters deplorably frivolous.

Chapter Sixteen

Half an hour afterwards the Inspector came in, carrying a black leather document case with a zipper. He brought with him a breath not exactly of fresh air, but of the salesmanlike substitute for it that seemed to surround him. He wasn't exactly like a salesman perhaps so much as a salesman's model, all those young men you see on showcards in chemists' shops who haven't got halitosis or dandruff or decaying teeth, and are therefore going to get the girl and the job. Perhaps the reason I noticed the Inspector's appearance so much was that it's rather like mine, except of course for my gammy leg.

"Mr Nelson." He came forward with a bright smile and a firm handshake. "Congratulations on your promotion."

"Thanks. You've got to hear of it pretty quickly."

"Good news travels fast." He uttered this cliché with a smile.

I thought I should say something solemn. "It's not so much promotion as finding someone to stand in for Willy. They've got this big new scheme on, and somebody's got to get behind it. I know the routine, so I'm Joe Soap."

"Yes, I understand that." He sat down, pulled up the knees of his trousers and seemed to regard me expectantly. Again I felt bound to say something.

"Is there anything fresh on Willie's death?"

"Anything fresh?" He seemed to consider this, look all round it you might say, before answering. "In a way, yes. Negative stuff, mostly. We haven't found anybody who saw anyone going in to or out of Strayte's flat that evening between the important times. We've found no taxi-driver who took a fare there or away from there, nobody in the street remembers a car being parked outside the place or anything like that. Negative, you see, but useful in a way. Police work's very dull, you get ten negatives to one positive. It's not much the kind of thing you write about in your mystery stories. Only I forgot, they aren't written, are they, they're dictated, and anyway you don't do it." I let all this pass without comment, but apparently he expected an answer. "Do you?"

"No. I explained that yesterday."

"So you did. But you do a bit sometimes, embroidering on the writer's work. That's so, isn't it?"

"Yes."

"Like this, for instance." He produced two or three pages of Donovan's Thorby Larsen effort, with the passage George Pacey had criticised as being too strong marked in red ink. "You wrote that."

George, I thought. My pal. As if he had guessed what I was thinking, the Inspector spoke again. "Mustn't blame Pacey, he wasn't letting you down. He told me he'd been a bit worried about you lately, you'd been putting such a lot of – um – powerful feeling into your embroidery, and I asked him to let me see a sample."

I made the stock answer to a stock criticism. "Don't blame us. We don't create a public demand, we supply it."

"I see what you mean. Still, I should hate to show this thing to a psychiatrist." He gave me his toothy smile. "Not that I can ever understand what those fellows are getting at, anyway. Wouldn't you say there seemed to be a sort of strong feeling about this extract, though?"

The way he kept staring at me made me feel odd. I managed a laugh. "Just a job well done, or badly done maybe. I could show you fifty pieces like it that I've done in the past year, and

I expect Willie Strayte did as many. Is that all, Inspector? I've got work to do."

"There's just one other little thing." I flattered myself I knew his technique now, and braced myself for what was coming. "We checked on that statement about your movements. That check was negative too."

I just didn't understand him. "Negative?"

He was staring hard at me as he undid the zipper of the document case. "Here's the report of an interview with James Joldin, bar attendant at the Select Wine Bar, Gongora Street. On duty Tuesday evening from 6 to 9.30. Can't remember anyone of your description talking to anyone like the woman called Christy between the times you gave. Can't be sure about it because the bar got fairly busy."

"He'll remember when he sees me."

"Tried the Gongora Residential Hotel. Dirty little place, dirty little man on duty. Name Frederick Morgan. Ten people registered that night, five couples. Four of them were false addresses when we checked them. You didn't sign the register."

"No, Christy signed it."

"Christy, yes. Morgan says he doesn't know any Christy, never heard the name."

I could feel the band round my forehead. "But he spoke to her, said hallo Christy."

"He tells it differently." He turned over to the last sheet. "This Christy now, you don't know her last name, don't know where she lives. We're trying to find her, but so far we've had no luck. There are two or three women of that name who operate in the district, but they tend to close up tighter than an oyster when we come round making enquiries of this sort. Don't want to get into trouble. Can't blame them really." Inspector Crambo put the papers back in his document case, zipped it up and said apologetically: "See what I mean, it's all checking and double checking and at the end you've got something negative. Nothing interesting at all."

Chapter Seventeen

That lunchtime I went to check on the Inspector's check. I didn't doubt that when I spoke to the barman at the Select Wine Bar and the little man at the hotel they would remember me, or if they didn't remember me they'd remember Christy. The Select was pretty busy that day, with men eating sandwiches and drinking sherry. The rabbit-nosed barman was there, the French clock under glass behind him. I ordered a ham sandwich and a glass of white wine, and he served me without a flicker of expression. "Thanks, Jack."

"The name is Jimmy."

"You said that to me a couple of nights ago, remember?"

"I'm saying it to people all the time, sir.

"But you remember that I came in.

"If you say so. Excuse me." He moved along the counter and I ate my ham sandwich.

When he came back I ordered another and said to him, "I met a woman in this bar and bought her a drink. Her name was Christy."

He looked hard at me then. "Somebody has been in here asking questions already. I told them I don't know anything, can't say you were here, can't say you weren't. That's fair enough, isn't it?"

"We were here from about a quarter to eight to a quarter to nine. I drank sherry and then Madeira, she drank port. You must remember."

He went on as if he had not heard. "I've been in a bit of trouble with the coppers once, and once is enough. What you don't know can't hurt you. I'm not saying you were here and I'm not saying you weren't, I just don't remember. That's fair enough, isn't it?"

"As fair as your best girl's black moustache", I said. I finished my wine, walked out and along to the Gongora Residential Hotel. There was nobody in the hall. The registration book was on the desk open, and I looked at it. Just as the Inspector had said there were five sets of names written there for the night before last. Since I didn't know Christy's writing none of them meant anything to me. I banged the bell on the desk and the little ferret-faced man came down. He didn't say anything, but I got a strong impression that he knew who I was. With the barman I hadn't been sure, but I felt certain that this man remembered me. There was recognition in the beady eyes, though it was quickly blotted out.

I said, "Good morning. I've lost a cigarette case, and I thought I might have left it here when I stayed a couple of nights ago. Did the room maid come across it?"

He took his time about answering. "Couple of nights ago? Don't remember you."

"You knew the woman who came in with me, soon after half past eight. You spoke to her, said hallo Christy."

"Christy? Don't know any Christy who was in here. What was her first name?"

That took me back for a moment, but I was sure Christy had been a first name. I told him so, and that I didn't know her surname.

He shook his head. "Don't know her."

"Then why did you say hallo to her?"

"You got the wrong hotel, mister."

"You've had the police round here already enquiring about her, haven't you? You're liable to get into trouble over this if you go on lying."

"Anybody gets into trouble it won't be me. What I told them is just the same as I'm telling you. We keep a register like they say we've got to. Anyone comes here they sign in that register. You sign it?"

"You know damned well I didn't. Christy signed it."

"Ah Christy, Christy, I'm sick of hearing about this Christy. First the police gabbing about her, now you. I tell you what I told them, I don't know any Christy. And now I see you I don't know you and I don't want to know you. I like to keep out of trouble, and you sound to me like trouble with a big T."

I left it at that. In fact I seemed to have no choice about leaving it at that. It had been a pretty poor alibi at the best, and without Christy it was no alibi at all. "Christy", I said aloud. "I've got to find Christy." And I had to persuade her to talk. I'd never realised before how much afraid people are of talking simply because they don't want to run any risk of getting into trouble.

Chapter Eighteen

Back in the office I found myself thinking about my own affairs instead of concentrating on *Crime Magazine.* I decided to go round the Gongora Street district that evening and see if I could find Christy, or anyone who'd talked to her or knew her. Then I began to think about the Kline-Ross file, and the more I thought about it the queerer its disappearance seemed. If Willie hadn't given it back and it was neither in his room nor his flat, somebody must have taken it. And if somebody had taken it the file must be connected with his death. The more I thought about it, in fact, the stranger it seemed to me that Willie should have wanted the file at all. I had explained it to myself by saying that he was digging out a story for *Crime Magazine,* but what had put him on to Kline-Ross in the first place? There might be nothing in it, but then again it might be important. I had outlined to Rose last night the idea that Willie had got hold of some information about one of our Section editors that he had used to blackmail himself into the editorial job. The Kline-Ross case might somehow be connected with this information.

I rang for Sandy Donovan, and told him I wanted him to work with me on something for *Crime Magazine.* He coloured up and stammered out something about being proud to do it. I told him somebody had said there might be something for us in the Kline-Ross murder case, which had taken place in 1923. I asked him to check on the case, turn in a report and get hold of any cuttings about it that he could find. I said that if there was anything in it he'd get the job of writing it.

He nodded solemnly. "I'll ask Research if they've got anything on it."

I said hurriedly, "I've checked and they haven't. You've got to go out on this, Sandy. Try the newspaper morgues and our lawyer boys. They'll put you on to some other sources if we need them." We had a pretty slick firm of lawyers who advised us about libel and obscenity risks, and they were going to have a lot of work to do on *Crime Magazine*.

Sandy said all right. He seemed a bit baffled. "What sort of a case is this, Mr Nelson – Dave?"

"It's a murder case. I told you."

"Yes, I know, but I mean it's not one of these things like the Heath case, is it, because if it is I'd – I don't think I'm the best person – "

I said patiently, "I don't know what sort of case it is, Sandy. That's why I asked you to find out."

"Yes, I see."

"And here's one to remember, Sandy. Don't turn down assignments before you know what they are. There's plenty of time to do that afterwards." He coloured again. "Let me have something on this as quickly as you can make it. Try and do it by tomorrow afternoon."

He said he would, and went out. I was sorry to raise his hopes about the story. I was sorry for him altogether. He was a nice boy, too nice to be any good to us.

Chapter Nineteen

That night I drank in the *Bricklayers' Arms* and the *Plough and the Stars* and the *Bundle of Hay,* which are all round about Gongora Street. A girl I met in the *Bundle of Hay* took me into Freddy's Caff because she knew a girl named Christy who was often in there. This girl proved to be a Swedish near-blonde named Greta Christiansen, but she had a friend who knew a Christy something or perhaps a something Christie over at the Blue Room. Christie wasn't at the Blue Room but I tracked her down in a basement club called the Major's Parlour where five Negroes got more noise out of saxophones, trumpets and drums than I would have thought possible. She was a nice girl that Christie, and obliging, but she was not the Christy I was looking for. Neither was Chris Martin, who drank a whisky with me in the *Bag o' Nails,* nor Molly Christie who drank a large port at my expense in the *Horseshoe,* nor horse-toothed Christie Carraway who thumped the piano at the Diving Bell. And some of these Christys and Christies and their men friends told me about others, all of them nice girls and on the game or at least willing to oblige. They were not around at this particular moment of this particular evening, but if I liked to hang around an hour or so they would be almost certain to drop in. I heard about Chris Anderson and Bella Christie who called herself a model, and Christy Freeman and Red Christie, Christie the soak and Chrissie Condon (who works for the moving pictures, they told me with a wink). And there were half a dozen others. Some of them I ruled out on the ground of age or appearance, but there were still too many who could have been my Christy. Nobody knew where these Christys and Christies lived, everybody said stick around and they'd turn up.

I stuck around for a long time. I talked to a man who thought I was the Press and offered to sell me his life story, in prison and out, for twenty pounds. I talked to a girl who said she could get me in to an exhibition for a couple of nicker. A man tried to give me shares in the Nova Zembla Gold Corporation, another man read me ten out of a series of a thousand sonnets he'd written.

I got home at half past one in the morning. I was full of whisky and gin and sandwiches and sausage rolls and port and sour red wine. I hadn't found my Christie or Christy. My head ached and the rubber band inside it seemed to have contracted a little. I felt miserably sober and very wide awake as I got into my cold and lonely bed.

Chapter Twenty

The most terrible part of a nightmare is the moment just before you wake up screaming. I woke with my own scream ringing in my ears. What had I dreamed? I could not remember, but I knew that there was something I should be afraid of. I heard the scrape of key in lock, and thought for some reason of brisk Inspector Crambo. There were steps across the hall, and the intensity with which I listened for them was painful. The steps reached the bedroom door. I sat up in bed and fumbled for the bedside light. There was a moment of terror while I searched for the switch, afraid that the door would open before I could turn on the light. Then the light was on and the door open, and Rose stood in the doorway. She was wearing a red raincoat that I thought she had given up years ago, and she looked as she had done when we first got married.

"You've come back."

"Yes." She took off the raincoat, under which she was wearing a skirt and jumper that I remembered from long ago.

"For good?"

"For as long as you want me." With a curious smile on her face she slipped quickly out of her clothes and put on a nightdress.

"I want you all the time. I've been looking for that woman Christy." I remembered that I hadn't told Rose about Christy, but she didn't seem to notice. Still with that fixed mechanical smile on her face she glided into bed and stretched out an arm to switch off the light.

I clasped her to me. There was something wrong, I knew that there was something wrong as I held her and felt the soft body changing under my hands, the silky hair turning to bristles sharp and wiry, the whole texture of the body hardening and growing colder. I felt again frantically for the light switch, couldn't find it. I tried to get free of the body that clung to me with serpentine insistence, its legs and arms twining round me in the thick darkness. It was not until I felt the coarse prickliness of a chin nuzzling my shoulder that I knew the thing in bed with me was not Rose but Willie Strayte. I sat up in bed, tore the thing's arms away from my neck, screamed at the top of my voice (but silently, silently), and tried once again to find the light switch that would show me what I was struggling with…

The most terrible part of a nightmare is the moment just before you wake up screaming. When you are once awake the apparatus of terror is seen to be so trivial – a pillow from which two or three feathers have come out, a sheet wound round the legs. And when you are awake you don't want to go back to sleep again, you dare not go back to sleep. If you can read a book you are lucky. If you can't read a book there is nothing to do but think.

Chapter Twenty-One

In the morning for some reason I felt much better. I made my own breakfast and ate it, and on the way to the office called in on a charwoman we sometimes employed, named Mrs Gaskin. She agreed to come in every morning to clean up when I told her that Rose was away for a few days. I reached the office almost jaunty, perturbed only by a small nick in my chin, shaving damage. I saw Sir Henry as I went in, and to my surprise the old man stopped me.

Leaning on his stick he gave me a pallid smile. "Good morning. Ah – Nelson, isn't it?"

"Dave Nelson, Sir Henry. Good morning."

"Mr – h'm – Dimmock was singing your praises to me recently. He assured me you were the very best man possible for our – ah – new project." It didn't seem right to confirm that, so I said nothing. "It is an – um – important project, Mr Nelson. Energy, enthusiasm, readiness for hard work will be needed and – above all new ideas, Mr Nelson, new ideas."

"We're looking out for those all the time, Sir Henry. Everybody's keen to see we get a magazine that's right on the mark."

"Yes. Yes." He looked at me with his watery eyes, tapped with his stick on the floor, seemed to be trying to think of something else to say. "Good morning, Mr Nelson."

In the office I looked at my desk pad and saw that Jenny Fisher, who did the general secretarial work of the Crime

Section, had suggested that I ought to have a general get-together with the writers about the new magazine. She was absolutely right, and I asked her to ring round and lay it on for eleven o'clock. Then I sat back and tried to concentrate on what I ought to say. It was no good. I had the feeling that there was something I should have noticed, some quite simple thing that would solve all my problems. We all have these feelings at some time or another, and generally they mean nothing at all. But I had the feeling, and it wouldn't go away.

Chapter Twenty-Two

So I called them in and talked to them. There were six of them. I've already mentioned Mary Speed and Netta Shuttlewort. Then there were four men, a little Jew named Solly Birkett who could turn out a very good line of Thorby Larsen stuff, our locked room expert Harold Paynter who was a middle-aged pain in the neck, and a couple of others named Seed and Milligan who did all kinds of stuff. The only one on duty that day and not there was Sandy Donovan and I was just going to ask where he'd got to when I remembered I'd sent him out to get stuff on the Kline-Ross case. George Pacey sat in on the conference too. Sitting in on conferences is a kind of occupation in a place like ours, where everything you do can turn out to be somebody else's business.

A few days earlier it had seemed to me that I had some lively ideas for *Crime Magazine*, but today I found myself waffling and rambling on in a dismal sort of way. They listened to me carefully, but I could hear George's foot tapping impatiently as I went over the ground that had been covered by Hep. Then we got down to cases. I put Solly Birkett on to the cartoon story, telling him to prepare enough stuff for a six months' run. All the men were keen to handle that, but I knew Solly would get more out of it than the others. Mary Speed was to handle the readers' correspondence, to start with the second issue. George and I both thought that was a feature that ought to be tied closely to whatever crimes there were a wave of at that particular time. If there's one thing you learn from studying the newspapers it is that crime waves are always with us.

But the real question was what story we were going to feature in the first issue. Solly Birkett wanted Jones and Hulten, Mary Speed said we should never get anything juicier than the case of the American Lonely Heart murderers Martha Beck and Raymond Fernandez. Paynter gabbled on about some Star Chamber inquisition case or other, Seed and Milligan who always seemed to work as a team wanted the Browne and Kennedy case. Netta Shuttleworth came up with two ideas – Peter Kurten the Dusseldorf mass murderer, and a new treatment of Jack the Ripper. We batted all this around for some time until George Pacey who'd been blowing clouds of pipe-smoke all over us, interrupted.

"Don't think we want to go too far along the line of pure sensation, if you know what I mean. Some of this stuff is interesting all right, but I'm not sure it's quite suitable."

"Just my own feeling," I said smoothly. I might have waffled a bit, but I wasn't going to let George take charge of what was really my party. "Tell you what I think. Jack the Ripper no, not unless you can get something really new on it, Netta. Too much written about it already, played out. Peter Kurten, not for the first number, though it's a hell of a good idea. I'd like you to rough something out for a later issue and let me see it. The first number ought to be something English and that lets out Lonely Hearts too, though that's something that ought to be written for number four or five. Star Chamber no, not for a top story, might make a second feature. Will you write it that way, Harold. That leaves us Jones and Hulten, Browne and Kennedy – and I'd like to add Rouse and Buck Ruxton. Mary, will you handle Rouse? It might be a case where you could use that technique of several first person narratives you were talking about? And Netta, will you take Buck Ruxton?"

"What shall I do with him?" Netta rolled her eyes. She was a blonde, big, hard and bony.

"Don't forget we're not going off half-cock on this. We want at least three top stories in hand when the first issue appears."

Soon after that the conference broke up, and I congratulated myself that after all I had handled it reasonably well. As they were going out Netta said, "Of course, we've got a top story on our doorstep. Why don't we run a feature story on Willie Strayte?"

There was silence. Then George Pacey took his pipe out of his mouth and said, "If that was good, I still wouldn't like it."

"I feel the same way", I said. "No, Netta."

She shrugged. "You're the boss. I didn't know we were running a course in ethics."

"We're not. But it's a dirty bird that fouls its own nest."

When the others had gone, George lingered. "How's it going?" I said all right. "Where's Donovan?"

"I sent him out on a research job. The Kline-Ross case", I added on impulse.

If the name meant anything to George he didn't show it. "I wanted to have a word about him. I don't see he belongs here, do you?"

Although I agreed with him, I felt a queer impulse not to say so. "Give him another week or two. He may settle down."

He made a face. "If you say so."

Chapter Twenty-Three

Sandy Donovan came into my office about twelve o'clock obviously delighted with himself, carrying a paper folder under his arm. He said to me reproachfully, "You really wanted to test me out on this one, didn't you, Mr Nelson – Dave?"

"What do you mean?"

"You left me to find out for myself that it wasn't British."

"Wasn't British?" I stared at him. "You mean the murder and the trial took place outside Britain."

"And the escape."

"The escape. Oh yes."

He looked surprised. "I thought the escape would be the point in it for us."

"Maybe it is. Let's have a look."

But Sandy wanted me to know how clever he'd been. "First I checked through all British trials for 1923 and a year backwards and forwards, and got nowhere. So I thought perhaps you were just kidding me on it. Then Jerry Eager suggested I should try other countries." Jerry Eager was one of the partners in that firm of solicitors I've mentioned, who worked for us. "He put me on to a chap named Macdonald, a sort of walking encyclopædia on murder cases. Macdonald had never heard of it, said it couldn't be of much interest. So then I worked on the names Kline and Ross, began to try the embassies – "

"Fine, Sandy, you've done a good job. Now just pass over what you've got."

He looked hurt, but he passed over the folder. "It was South Africa. I got hold of a chap named Voigt who had a collection of old South African newspapers. I had a job, I can tell you, to get him to part with them for a few days. He won't let them out of his sight longer than that."

I opened the folder, which contained several yellowed copies of the *East Transvaal Standard* for June 1923.

"The important thing for us", Sandy said, "is that George and Alec Ross escaped after sentence. I suppose that's what you had in mind."

I said decisively, "That's all for now, Sandy. Come back in half an hour."

At last he went out and I settled down to read the papers. The *East Transvaal Standard* was published twice weekly, and six of the eight issues covered the three weeks from June the third to June the twenty-fourth. The two others were a few weeks later. From the papers I put together the pieces of a simple story in which someone named Ross had killed someone named Kline. That was the essence of it, but the details had a certain interest.

Max Kline and George Ross were both wildcat prospectors in the Transvaal. They had come out at the end of the war and like a lot of others had existed on the borderline of hunger while they waited for a lucky strike. Perhaps because of the fact that they had arrived more or less together, the two men had become friends although they apparently had little in common. Kline was of mixed German-Dutch origin, Ross was believed to be Scottish. Kline worked alone, Ross was helped by his sixteen-year-old half-brother Alec. Kline was married to a woman nearly twenty years younger than himself, Ross was a bachelor.

The Ross brothers were made welcome at Kline's house, until Kline apparently became suspicious of the relations between his wife Carlotta and George Ross. At a local haunt named Mac's Bar Kline had a fight with George Ross, and although Ross was the younger man he had a good deal the worst of it, according to witnesses. "They fought for near half an hour, and Maxie knocked him stone cold", said one of them named David Greener at the trial. "And nobody was sorry. Ross had been treating Maxie the dirtiest way a man can treat another who takes him into his home." Asked how he knew about this, Greener said everybody knew it, everyone but Maxie.

As I read I began to get an image of Max Kline as the simple good-natured giant type, a bit light in the brain box. I turned to his picture in the paper and there he was, beetle-browed, rock-jawed and stolid, with that look of incipient idiocy that good-natured men who work with their hands often have.

After the fight George Ross had wiped the blood off himself and said nothing but his young half-brother Alec, who bad with difficulty been stopped from joining in, threatened Kline. Witnesses differed about just what he said, but it was something about looking out for himself on dark nights and something else about making his will because he very likely wouldn't live long. Kline apparently didn't take any notice, and nobody else took much notice either. It was the kind of thing that can mean anything or nothing according to who says it, and everyone who heard it knew that Alec Ross had a big mouth.

I had another couple of images now, of Alec Ross as a raw boastful boy and of his elder half-brother George as a man close, sly and somehow mean. I looked at the blurred photographs on the paper's front page, and saw that these two also ran pretty true to type. Alec Ross had rather nondescript, unformed features, but there was a reckless look in his eye. He had a general look of being the kind of boy who'd be happy taking away a chocolate from a baby. His half-brother George was much older, in his forties perhaps. He was tight-lipped, hatchet-faced and crafty, the sort who'd fling his money about like a man with no hands. By the side of George Ross was a picture of Carlotta, the cause of all the trouble. Like most women who cause trouble she looked like nothing at all. The head and shoulders picture showed a woman with big shoulders and a face like a pudding. The shapeless nose in the middle of it might have been the plum.

Kline still went down to Mac's Bar regularly, and a week after the row he was there until ten o'clock. Neither George nor Alec Ross was in the bar. Kline left to walk the mile back to his home, which led through the streets and then over a field. In the field he was savagely battered to death. He was found the next morning, and the same day the Ross brothers were arrested. They were on their way out of town to make a strike somewhere else, they said, having given up hope of doing any good in Arenburg, which was the name of the place where all this happened. Stuffed under the floorboards of their shack the police found a pair of George Ross' trousers and Alec's work jacket. Both were heavily stained with blood.

The trial didn't take long. The Ross brothers had no alibi for the night of the murder after ten o'clock. They were proved to have been lying when they said they were at home all the evening. In fact two witnesses, one of them the same Greener who had been present at the fight, saw them drinking in another bar. Carlotta went into the witness box and agreed that she had been George's mistress, but maintained that George had never made any threats about her husband. The Rosses' explanation of the blood on the trousers and jacket was that Alec had cut his arm badly at work, and that George had got some of the blood on his trousers. They didn't want to take the bloodstained things with them, so they left them in their shack. It was true that Alec had cut his arm, but a doctor testified that it was a month-old cut, whereas the blood was fresh. When asked why they had put the clothes under the floorboards of their shack, neither of the Rosses could offer an answer.

It was a straightforward enough case and the jury didn't take much time about finding them both guilty of murder. George was sentenced to death and Alec, in view of his youth, to twenty years' imprisonment. Three days after the sentence the brothers escaped from Arenburg which seemed to have been a fairly homey little place. The escape, like the rest of the story, was pretty simple. Alec had complained of violent stomach pains and an unsuspecting warder had opened his cell. Alec had knocked out the warder, opened George's cell and let him out, jumped on and tied up the other warder on duty, and the two of them had walked out of jail. After that they had vanished, or at least they had never been recaptured. The last two copies of the paper contained brief reports of the way in which the police were continuing their enquiries. The brothers were reported in Johannesburg, two men had been arrested in Cape Town on suspicion of being the Rosses and then released, they were said to have boarded boats to England, Germany, the United States.

That was the Kline-Ross case and that was the way, at least in these newspaper reports, that the case ended.

Chapter Twenty-Four

I thought about it and tried to see what Willie Strayte could have found in it. There were several possibilities.

The first was that I'd simply invented the idea that the Kline-Ross case had any connection with Willie's death. According to this theory Willie had heard somebody mention the case, discovered that we had some stuff on it, got the file up and then lost or mislaid it. That was what you might call the common-sense view, the view that would appeal to Inspector Crambo, but somehow it wasn't a view I could take. It was easy to say the file had got mislaid, but in practice that just wouldn't have happened. Nobody would have been likely to take it out of Willie's office, and if it had been taken out innocently Miss Richards would have found it by now. Apart from that, the story was a commonplace one, with nothing in it for us. If Willie had heard about it he would have recognised that immediately. Or a glance through the file would have been enough. I was convinced, though it might not be easy to pass on my conviction to anybody else, that Willie had wanted this file for some purpose which had nothing to do with *Crime Magazine* or one of our books.

So far so good. Somehow Willie had got on to the Kline-Ross case. He had discovered that it was connected with somebody in our office. He had tried to profit by the discovery, and he had been killed doing so. When he was killed the file had been taken away. That was the view to which I was committed, and the more I thought about it the more I liked it.

Where did I go from there? It struck me that if this had been a detective story I should have found out from the newspaper cuttings that some quite different person had killed Kline – his wife, for instance – and that would have given me some kind of lead. But there was no doubt at all that the Ross brothers had killed him. I thought about but rejected such unlikely ideas as the possibility that Kline had had a son who had come to England seeking revenge, and settled down on a solution which, you may say, was fairly obvious from the start.

Alec Ross had come to England. At some time or another he had joined Gross Enterprises and become one of the Section editors. In some way Willie Strayte had found this out. He had blackmailed Alec Ross with the threat that he would reveal his identity so that Alec would be sent back to serve his prison sentence. The first gentle turn of the screw had forced Alec to cast a vote against me in the election so that Willie got the editorial job. Then Willie had applied the next turn of the screw, and that had been a mistake. Willie had been killed.

Why should it have been Alec Ross and not George? Well, there was the question of age. Alec Ross would now be in his late forties, but George would be a very old man, much too old to be on our editorial staff. And from the newspaper reports I got the impression that Alec was really the moving spirit in the murder, in spite of his youth. It was he who had made the threat to Kline, which seemed idle but was in fact carried out. It was he who had knocked out one warder and tied up another. Looking at the old photographs I felt that Alec Ross might be capable of any rashness, whereas George would always be meanly circumspect.

I congratulated myself upon my clear-headed logical approach at the time, but I daresay I was influenced unconsciously by the fact that Alec Ross fitted my ideas, whereas George Ross didn't. I went over the Section editors in my mind, for age. George Pacey said he was forty-five, Bill Rogers looked fifty, Charles Peers was in his early forties, Hep was perhaps a year or two younger.

They were all possible, just. Only Clem Bennett of Romance seemed definitely too young, a smooth-faced chap in his late thirties like me.

But you can narrow it down a bit more than that, Dave boy, I told myself. The man who stopped me from getting the editorial job was one who should have voted *for* me. I had reckoned on a no from Hep, and maybe from Clem Bennett too. My three firm voters were George Pacey, Bill Rogers and Charles Peers. One of these three had voted against me, and that one was Alec Ross. I looked at the photograph and tried to imagine its transformation into each of the three men. The effort defeated me. The photograph didn't look like any of them, but then how many photographs of boys are recognisable a great many years later?

The trouble with any series of deductions of this kind is that there always comes a moment when the whole thing seems preposterous. Quite suddenly this moment arrived for me, when I stared at the indistinct photograph in the *East Transvaal Standard*. I found myself tearing the whole spider-web that I had painstakingly constructed, and making all sorts of absurd and irrelevant suppositions about it. Among them was one which seemed disturbingly possible. Supposing there was some kind of statute of limitations which meant that after so many years had passed Alec Ross could not be sent back to prison? That at least, I reflected as I got on the telephone to Jerry Eager, was a problem I could resolve. If Jerry said that Alec Ross couldn't be sent back to prison it was goodbye to my theory.

The telephone girl said, "Here's Mr Eager for you."

"Jerry. This is Dave Nelson."

"Hallo, Dave. How's crime?"

"Having a little trouble with it at the moment. We've got a story on our hands that doesn't seem to be working out right.

Fellow in it is being blackmailed on account of a crime he committed thirty or forty years back."

"What sort of crime?"

"Murder. It's the central situation, and it's got to be right. Is it plausible that somebody should be blackmailing this respectable gentleman with the threat of revealing his part in a murder that old?"

"Part in it? You said murder just now."

"Murder I meant. Got myself a bit mixed."

"This takes place in England, I suppose?"

"Well, that can make a difference. Where was it?"

"Could be one of three or four places. At the moment we've got it fixed on South Africa."

"I see." Whatever it was Jerry Eager saw it seemed to change the tone of his voice. "Was anyone put on trial for this murder?"

"Yes. I forgot to tell you that. This chap was put on trial, found guilty and sentenced, but he escaped."

"I see", Jerry said again. "You seem to have a good enough story there."

"You mean he could be taken back to South Africa?"

"You didn't say he'd left it."

"Hell no, that's something else I forgot. The action of the story takes place in England, though the crime was in South Africa."

"Yes. It's all right as a hypothetical story." Then Jerry added carefully, "If it's that hypothetical."

"How do you mean?"

"I had much the same enquiry a few days ago about this hypothetical story. From Willie Strayte."

I said slowly, "You mean Willie put this same question to you, about a man being sent back to South Africa after being found guilty of murder."

"Yes. I'd be a little careful of making investigations on my own if I were you, Dave. The police are pretty good at that sort of thing."

"Hell, Jerry, I said this was all hypothetical. You know I've taken over Willie's work."

"I know. Sandy Donovan was round here this morning making some enquiries on this same hypothetical line, or am I wrong?"

"Quite wrong", I said firmly. "Thanks a lot, Jerry."

"No trouble at all."

I put back the receiver with confidence surging up in me. I had the feeling now that I was really on to something. If Willie Strayte had been asking the same questions that I was asking, it meant that I was following just his line of thought. Willie had learnt from Jerry Eager that his information would send Alec Ross back to South Africa to serve his sentence. Then he had set to work to use this information, and in using it he had got himself killed. I had demonstrated this now to my own satisfaction. That left me with two questions to answer. *One,* how had Willie discovered the identity of Alec Ross? *Two,* which of the three suspects really was Alec Ross – George Pacey, Bill Rogers or Charles Peers? I put the first question aside as too difficult to answer at the moment, and concentrated on the second.

At that point I began to have doubts about my three candidates. I've described George Pacey, a typical little English businessman, good at his work, fond of his wife and two children and his decent suburban home. As far as I knew George had never been out of England, except perhaps during the war. He might have played me a dirty trick over the election, but it took a lot of imagination to see him as violent, reckless young Alec Ross.

When I passed on to Charles Peers the amount of imagination required seemed to turn the whole idea into fantasy. Charles Peers was a type – there's always somebody more or less like him in an organization like ours. He wore huge horn-rimmed glasses, stooped a bit, and liked to talk about things like the ritual significance of dance. He was said to be a good Science Fiction editor. I got on with him fairly well. He used to look at me through the horn rims as if I were something that had just dropped in from Mars, and I felt more or less the same way about him. I didn't make the mistake of thinking Charles Peers was just another long-haired intellectual – he was vague about a lot of things and then surprisingly shrewd when you least expected it – but I just couldn't see him as young Alec Ross.

That left Bill Rogers, the obvious candidate. By his own admission he had lived abroad for a long time. He talked a lot about America, and he might easily have gone there after he and his half-brother escaped from South Africa. He never talked about his early life in any detail. He was round about the right age. There could be no doubt about it, Bill Rogers filled the bill reasonably well. Yet somehow I couldn't feel happy about the idea that he was the right man. About Alec Ross, in those newspaper reports, there was something wild, forceful and genuine whereas Bill, as I've said, always impressed me as very much of a phoney.

Nevertheless, I decided, Bill ought to be investigated and Charles Peers and George Pacey should be investigated too. An echo of what Netta Shuttleworth had said occurred to me, and in spite of what I'd said to her I thought it would be a hell of a story if I could trace a murderer inside our own organization. Pretty disastrous in a way, o doubt, but not half so disastrous as having that slick Inspector Crambo pin something on *me.*

I had reached this point when the door opened and Sandy Donovan pushed his head round it. "I wondered what you thought about that case."

"The case? Oh, Kline-Ross. I've read it through. You've done a good job in getting hold of it, Sandy, but I don't think there's anything in it for us."

He mumbled in disappointment. "Thought I had an idea on it that I might try to develop. For the magazine."

"What was that?"

"If I could retell the story in the paper, there's something very vivid in the way they put it, the way the evidence is given I mean, and give some description of the background, the kind of life they lived over there I mean. It seems to have been pretty tough and might be interesting to read about, and then I could end up with the question what happened to George and Alec Ross? I thought it might make an interesting story." He blurted it out almost all in a breath and added hastily, "not a lead story of course, I didn't mean that, just one of the shorter pieces."

Where can you begin with a boy who just doesn't understand the elements of what's needed, what can you say to him? I drew a deep breath, counted ten, let it out and then told him as gently as I could. "That wouldn't do for us, Sandy. The emphasis for our readers in a story like that would have to be first of all on George Ross' relations with Carlotta Kline, and then we should have to play up some contemporary angle if we could find one. The rest of it is just the leisurely sort of stuff you can find in a novel, it hasn't got the zip we want."

"Oh yes. Yes, I see." But I knew he didn't see at all. He held out his hand for the papers but I told him I'd hang on to them for a day or so. The telephone rang and it was Charles Peers. He asked me in his solemn way whether I was free to have lunch with him. I told him I was, and spent most of the half hour to lunchtime wondering what he wanted to see me about. Since I wanted to do a little digging into his past anyway, I regarded the telephone call as rather handy.

Chapter Twenty-Five

"A very interesting article by Mildred Forster in the *Psychoanalytical Recorder*", Charles Peers said. "Controverting Reich's theories of orgone energy."

I stabbed at my stewed steak. "Is that so?"

"Reich believes, as you know, that all human beings are infused with cosmic energy which is then discharged by them through the orgasm. A constant process of refuelling, you might say, goes on, which is in fact responsible for the continuance of life on the planet. But – this is the important thing – Reich believes that the colour of this orgone energy is blue. Mildred Forster sets out to show that it is red. And she has linked the concept of the redness of orgone energy with an entirely new circular theory of personality."

I grunted. Inside my head I felt the rubber band expanding and contracting.

"Mildred's theory is based on the infinite capacity and adaptability of the infant mind. The circle of actions that may seem 'natural' to the infant, she says, is boundless, because its concepts have not been compressed and distorted by the taboos of what we call civilised living. For the small child the possibilities of mind and imagination – of the personality, in fact – have no limits whatever. Mildred conceives the creation of the adult personality as a narrowing-down of the possibilities inherent in the infant mind. I am repressed, therefore I am. Every new taboo imposed by adults and by tradition narrows the circle of the personality. Our actions move within a narrowing circle of possibilities, more and more things are forbidden us by the myths that we elevate into systems of ethics. We are like goldfish swimming in an ever-contracting bowl."

Now the band was tight, now it was released with an almost painful twang. Somewhere behind the band lay a headache. "What happens in the end?"

"There is no *end,* that is a vulgar conception. We spend our lives swimming round the bowl, trying vainly to enlarge it. If we are lucky it stays the same size as it was in youth, but for most of us it narrows every five years with a fresh surge of intolerance and insensitivity. The only people for whom there is an *end* are the misfits of society, extreme psychopaths for whom the circle has been so narrowed by repression that only one action appears possible. The complications of life have been eliminated for them by the destruction of choice. The paranoiac *knows* that his hostility to others is justified by their persecution of him, the psychopathic homosexual *knows* that he can act in no other way than he does, the schizophrenic murderer *knows* that he must direct all his cunning to the destruction of his beloved enemy. The circle of the personality has disappeared and become – a point." Peers jabbed his fork at me. My head throbbed painfully. "A remarkable woman, Mildred. Do you know her?"

That seemed an opportunity. "She's German, isn't she?"

"Austrian."

"Oh yes. Did you meet her in Vienna?"

"Certainly not. At a party in Golders Green."

"I thought you spent some time in Vienna before the war." Vienna was a long way from South Africa, but it was a start.

"Whatever has given you that idea?" Charles Peers' spectacles had slid down his nose, and he peered at me now over the top of them.

"Can't remember who told me. Do you mean you've never been there?"

"I was there for a fortnight just before the *Anschluss.*"

"Funny, I could have sworn – but you've done a lot of foreign travel, haven't you, Charles? I always think of you as the best-travelled man of my acquaintance."

"Do you really? Then you can't have many acquaintances."

I was pushing it a little, but I thought I might as well go on. "Do you mean to tell me that's the only time you've been out of England?"

"I didn't say that at all." He gave me one of those glances that made me feel like a test-tube specimen. "Why are you so interested in my taste for foreign travel, Dave?"

"Pardon me, is my curiosity showing? When I discover the most-travelled-man in our organization I'm going to pin a Nelson medal on him."

"A bit of intelligence work in North Africa during the war's about my limit. You'd better ask Bill Rogers to tell you the story of his life." He looked round the pub we were lunching in and then said casually, "As a matter of fact, it's a sort of travelling I wanted to talk to you about."

I resigned myself to the fact that I probably shouldn't get any more out of him for the moment, and settled down to listen to what he had to say, trying at the same time to ignore what was now a positive headache. At least he wasn't talking about orgone energy and the circular theory of personality any more. But knowing Charles Peers I knew that he was incapable of making a straightforward approach to any subject – he was just about as circular, or circuitous in that respect as it's possible to be. Pushing back a lank piece of hair that had strayed down somewhere near his nose he said, "How do you fancy a space-time journey to Jupiter? It's a serious project."

"What's that?" After a moment I realised that he was joking, though I didn't appreciate the joke. When people are making a joke I like them to laugh, but Charles Peers looked more solemn than usual.

"Tell me seriously again, what do you think of the prospects of *Crime Magazine?*"

There was only one answer to that. "First rate. Don't you?"

"You're absolutely happy with it? Receiving your full quota of orgone energy?"

I thought I saw what he was getting at. I ordered biscuits and cheese and cut the cheese deliberately into half. "If you mean I ought not to have taken the job because of Willie's death I can only say I don't agree with you. There's a job to be done, and if they think I'm the best man to do it that's up to them."

"That's not what I meant. As a matter of fact if it had rested with me alone you'd have got the job in the first place." He had pushed back the great horn-rimmed glasses into place. Behind the pebbled lenses I could not see his eyes but I felt that he was weighing me up, deciding whether to say any more or not. "A change of air is sometimes a good thing and I don't mean necessarily a change of interplanetary air – though really one shouldn't talk about air in relation to interplanetary travel." He arranged a fork and spoon at right angles. "In your case particularly, I should have thought – do I make myself clear?"

I simply hadn't an idea of what he was talking about, and didn't know what to say, so I said nothing.

He put fork and spoon neatly together. "I didn't care for that Inspector chap, did you? I should say there's a dangerously narrowed personality at work there, painfully compressed and with only one very evident end in view, eh?"

I still said nothing.

"Can you come round and have a drink at my flat tonight, about seven? We can continue this interesting little discussion there. 83 Willis Gardens, just off the King's Road."

I said I should like to. The waiter brought the bill. Charles Peers looked at it with his glasses pushed well down on his nose. "Shall we make this a Dutch lunch?"

He may have been a bit unworldly in his conversation but he was all there when it came to money. Reluctantly I took out a ten-shilling note, and got half a crown change. I can't say I felt the seven and sixpence had been exactly well spent, but at least I was certain of one thing. Unless those newspaper reports had been even more inaccurate than usual, Charles Peers was not Alec Ross.

Chapter Twenty-Six

Back in the office I dispelled the raw clamour of my headache with a sodium amytal tablet, sent it back to a place in my skull where it murmured quietly instead of roaring. I wondered why I had accepted Peers' invitation to a drink. Hadn't I got more important things to do? I had a feeling that I ought to do something about the Gongora Hotel, a feeling that while the barman at the Select Wine Bar really didn't remember me, the clerk at the Gongora knew perfectly well who I was and who Christy was. Indeed, hadn't she said so? But on thinking about it I found I couldn't be sure. The tablet had blurred the headache, but it seemed also to have blurred the edges of my recollection, so that a kind of mist was set between me and everything that had happened on the evening before Willie Strayte's death. Or was it just that I couldn't bear to think of the time before I knew about Rose and Willie Strayte?

Time and again during the afternoon my eye moved to the telephone on the desk. I could pick up the telephone, ask for a number, and perhaps speak to Rose. And when I spoke to her, what should I say? Come back to me, come back to me. A jingle formed itself in my head:

> Pink sugar princess, come back to me,
> Come back to me, come back to me,
> And I will eat you up.
> Your red sugar mouth and your blue sugar eyes

And under the frock your sugary thighs.
Oh sugar princess, come back to me
And I will eat you up.

I went back to the flat, took off my jacket and lay down on the bed staring up at a crack in the ceiling. The headache had begun again, the band was clamped tightly round my forehead. I felt a sudden and unusual need for a cigarette, got up and took one out of a box we kept in the sitting room. Then I felt in my pocket for my lighter, a rather unusual affair with a special all-weather lighting device, which Rose had given me one Christmas long ago. She smoked a good deal more than I did and it was a standing joke between us – at that time we had standing jokes – that neither of us ever had any matches. So she had bought me this lighter and had an inscription put inside the top: *D from R, Lighting Up Time.*

I was supposed to keep the lighter in my pocket but I often forgot to do so, and it wasn't there now. I had a fairly thorough hunt through the flat without finding the lighter. The whole place was looking much tidier after Mrs Gaskin's attentions, and I decided that she'd put the lighter in some pet place of her own, or perhaps I had even left it at the office. I used a match, smoked my cigarette, and went to the chest-of-drawers to get a clean shirt. After opening the drawer I stood staring down at the things it contained. Everything was there that should have been there – shirts, collars, vests and pants – but they were not in the right order.

Somebody had opened that drawer very recently, I was quite sure of that, although I couldn't have given reasons that would have satisfied Inspector Crambo. I'm not a very observant man in relation to most household things but I have always looked after my own clothes, even putting them away in the drawer myself when they came back from the laundry. So now I was quite certain that the grey shirt which should have been on top was underneath a blue one, and that the shirt collars were at the back of the drawer instead of being round about the middle as they should have been. I went through the drawer quickly to see if anything had been taken, but it hadn't. Then I stood staring at the blue shirt on top of the grey one.

It is hard to convey how shocked I felt at the idea that some stranger had been into the flat and had searched the chest of drawers. In theory Mrs Gaskin might have opened it, but she had worked for us now for three years and I had never known her do such a thing. In theory Rose might have come back to the flat, but even if she had I couldn't believe that she would have opened my clothes drawer which she never touched from one end of the year to another.

Leaving the chest of drawers open I went through the flat looking for other signs of an intruder. I didn't find any, but as I say about most things I am not an observant man. Slight changes in the positions of tables, cushions and so on would pass me by. It did seem to me that there was possibly some alteration in, of all places, a cupboard under the kitchen sink where we kept old beer and spirit bottles.

But I might have been wrong about this, and anyway Mrs Gaskin could have done it. I looked at the Yale lock outside the door and thought I saw scratches on it, but then again these scratches might have been days or even weeks old.

I went back again and looked at the blue shirt on top of the grey one, and wondered if I was quite right in the head. A queer sort of breaking and entering, in which nothing had been taken. And than I remembered my cigarette lighter. Supposing they had taken that, I asked myself, what would they have wanted it for? *Easy,* I answered, *they took it to leave on the scene of a crime.* Once you have begun this question and answer technique it's very difficult to stop. The crime in this case has already been committed. *But another crime may be in hand.* You're letting your imagination run away with you, Nelson. *Don't be too sure of that, hasn't the whole of this case shown that somebody is trying to frame me?* Has it, Nelson – or has it shown that you've got a well-developed persecution complex? Aren't you going to look a little foolish when you find that lighter on your desk tomorrow? Couldn't you have changed over those shirts yourself? *No.* I answered angrily, *No, no, no.*

Coming out of the question and answer game with an effort, I found myself still staring at the open drawer. I said aloud, "To hell with it", took out the grey shirt with the ridiculous feeling that I was destroying a vital piece of evidence, got another suit out of the wardrobe, and went into the bathroom.

A little more than half an hour later, freshly bathed and shaved, wearing the grey shirt and a newly-pressed suit, my headache held at bay by two more sodium amytal tablets, I was on my way to 83 Willis Gardens.

Chapter Twenty-Seven

Charles Peers' flat was very much what I'd expected. It took up the first floor of an early Victorian house, the furniture was all fairly new, there were half a dozen imitation Calder mobiles in the form of moons, suns and planets moving about in the living room. "The shapes of things to come", Charles said, Staring at me through the great pebbled glasses. "And this is my wife; Messalina."

A dark stumpy woman appeared at his side. "My name's not really Messalina, it's Jezebel. Charles only calls me Messalina as a pet name."

She said it perfectly seriously, and it wasn't for a few minutes that I realised she'd been joking and that her name was Jane. As I say I like people to laugh when they make a joke.

"Somebody you know", Charles Peers said. Mary Speed came out of a corner by the window where she'd been talking with a man. She smiled at me brightly, and I wondered again whether I ought to test out my idea that she had a thing about me.

The man was a big bald fellow wearing a fancy waistcoat. Mary turned to him and said, "My husband Bob, Dave Nelson."

Charles gave me a drink. Mary said, "Take the look of stupor off your face, Dave, I've told you before that I had a husband. Didn't you believe me?" I said something about her name. "It's Mary O'Kelly really, Speed's my maiden name, but it sounds more like a crime writer. At least that's what Bob thought, and what he thinks is generally right."

"Mary Speed", the bald man said in a rich voice. "It's got something. Mary O'Kelly now, that's just a bit of old Irish shamrock."

Mary asked me where Rose was. That came as a slight shock, I couldn't get it into my head that other people didn't know she'd left me. I said she'd had to go out, and I daresay I said it unconvincingly from the look Mary gave me.

Apart from that the conversation wasn't exactly sparkling, and there was no sign at all that Charles Peers meant to take up the subject we'd been talking about at lunch, whatever the subject was. I got the impression that he was waiting for something to happen, and also that he was nervous. He talked in very much his usual way, about creating films from visual images instead of from scripts, and about rewriting the history of Europe in terms of transport, but it seemed to me that his heart wasn't in it. His wife Jane or Jezebel or Messalina or whatever her name was sat at his feet looking adoringly up at him. Mary chimed in with a remark now and then, and her big bald husband (I remembered he was a BBC announcer) downed a couple of drinks and looked bored. I didn't blame him.

After a bit I gave up wondering what I'd been asked for and began to brood about Rose. When I came to think of it I had several things to brood about, Rose and the shirt in the wrong place and finding Christy and the Kline-Ross case, and I brooded away quietly while Charles Peers talked. Suddenly and quite involuntarily I found myself saying something instead of thinking it. What I said was: "Have any of you heard the name of Alec Ross?"

Charles Peers stopped talking. His spectacles had slipped down and his eyes, small and brown, looked at me over them with an expression of apparently genuine puzzlement. Mary knitted her forehead in a frown and stared hard at me. It was her husband who broke the silence.

"Why yes, there was an Alec Ross who used to work with me in Anglo-Asian films. Still does work there I believe. Kind of a contact man between us and the Chinese and Japs. Dark young chap, about thirty. That the one you mean?"

"That's not the one." I said with emphasis, "My Alec Ross spent some time in South Africa."

Mary said in her precise voice, "But why should you suppose we know anything about him, Dave?"

I looked at their faces, which gave me no information. And how foolish of me to have expected any. Noting Mary's guarded glance at her husband I saw myself holding tightly to the dock while she said, in that same precise voice: *Yes, he had been behaving strangely for several days. I remember one evening when we were having a drink at Mr Peers' flat...*

The sodium amytal had pushed back the headache again. My head felt full of cottonwool. A bell rang, and Charles Peers jumped up to answer it. He came back in a minute or two with a tubby twinkling-eyed little man whom he introduced to us as Jake Beverley.

"Well well", said Beverley as he shook hands with O'Kelly. "So you're Mr O'Kelly. Have a cigar." He took out a large gold-edged cigar case and O'Kelly accepted a fat brown cylinder.

"And Mary Speed, otherwise Mrs O'Kelly", said Charles Peers.

"Glad to know you," Beverley pushed his mottled nose close to Mary Speed's face. His small eyes twinkled at her.

Then it was my turn. My hand was encased in a mass of flesh tight but slightly damp, the nose was pushed at me, the eyes twinkled, two stars in a fleshy firmament. "Have a cigar."

"Thank you, I never smoke them."

"Cigarette." Another case appeared, all gold this time. Slightly hypnotised I took a cigarette and bent my head towards the flame of a gold lighter.

"What are you drinking?" Charles Peers asked. "Whisky, gin, sherry?"

"Glass of milk." Beverley patted his great stomach. "Got an ulcer. Wouldn't think it to look at me, would you, but there you are. With me everything turns to poison. Take a drink, eat a bit of steak and I'm in torture. Can't even smoke my own cigars. And mind you, I'm a man who likes his food and drink."

"That must be terrible." Charles Peers' manner, I noticed with surprise, was both fawning and earnest. Through the cottonwool in my head I sensed that Jake Beverley was somebody of importance.

"A man in my position, he's got to expect it. It's the money. There it is passing through my hands all the time, today it's here, tomorrow it's gone, next day it's back again double. My psychiatrist says it sets up tension, what do you expect he says living in a state of tension, but an ulcer. Get rid of the tension, get rid of the ulcer. What you mean, I said to him, is get rid of my money, and a few visits to you and I shall have passed over a wad of it. That's psychiatrists for you all over, never seen men so keen about money."

"You're in the City." I said it more as a statement than a question.

"I'm everywhere", Jake Beverley said simply. "In the City, but a dozen other places too. Look for cashola and you'll find me. I attract it, with me it's magnetism like some people have got second sight." He sipped his glass of milk with an expression of some distaste. "And is it worth it, that's what I ask myself? When all's said and done it's the simple things that count in life. Give a man a hundred thousand pounds, take away sight, taste and hearing and what good does it do him? That's my philosophy, and always has been."

Charles Peers and his wife were listening with the most devout attention. Is that what we've been asked here for, I wondered, to hear this self-made ulcer victim talk about his philosophy?

"Charlie here tells me you work with him in this little book business, is that right?"

It was the first time I'd ever heard anybody call Charles Peers Charlie. Mary and I nodded our heads like sheep.

"Books now, I like books. 'A good book is the life blood of a master spirit.' I read that once in a book. Struck me, that phrase did, though I'm not a reading man myself. I always say you can live or you can read, no time for both." A mass of blubber, I thought, a mass of blubber with a line of blabber. Even as I thought this Beverley's voice, oily but grating, like a machine running slightly out of true, said "Been having a spot of bother there, I understand."

It was Charles Peers who answered. "Willie Strayte was killed. One of our Executive Editors."

"I saw something about it, though I don't often look at the papers. Are you one of these Executive Editors too, Davy boy?"

"I'm an Executive Editor. If it matters."

"How about you, Mary? Another of the same?"

"I'm a writer", Mary said meekly. "That means I do the donkey work and Dave supervises my stuff."

From the tubular-armed chair that he filled Beverley held up a thick soft hand with three rings on it. "The details I don't want to know, the details I leave to other people. Just the general picture is all I want."

The room was blue with cigar smoke, and I felt as though half the smoke in the room were inside my head. I spoke irritably. "I don't see why you want any sort of picture."

Beverley took a sip of his milk and looked hard at me "Didn't you tell him, Charlie boy?"

Charles Peers coughed apologetically, and pushed his glasses up on his nose. "We talked over things in general at lunch today. I didn't mention names, but I think I can say Dave and I were agreed in principle."

"I don't know what you're talking about", I said, though by this time I was beginning to get an idea.

Beverley spread out his hands. "I don't blame you. Charlie here is a clever boy, but sometimes he wraps things up so fancy you got to be Einstein to understand them. Now I always like to put my cards face up on the table where anyone can see them, so the other man knows what I've got. And I expect him to do the same by me. That's what I call square dealing. And if everyone had dealt as square by me as I have by them let me tell you I should have my fleet of gold-plated Rollses by now." He looked round at us all in an injured manner. "You be square with me, Davy boy, and I'll be square with you. There's a possibility – don't put it higher than that, mind, but there's a genuine possibility – I might be coming into the book business. Your sort of book business, I mean, that's the only one I'm interested in. Educational and profitable too. And if I come in it will be in a big way. I shall want people, and I want good people. Charlie boy tells me you're both good. That's enough for me. Whatever you're getting now I raise it by fifty per cent. There are my cards on the table, face up like Jake Beverley always plays them. How does it sound, good or bad, yes or no?"

"Good", said Mary Speed. I said nothing.

"Let's hear from you, Davy boy."

"I don't know." Through the haze of cigar smoke and the haze in my head I tried to puzzle it out. "I don't see how it makes sense. You say you're coming into our kind of book business, and coming in in a big way. That means there'll be three firms running in the multiple author book market, Gross Enterprises, Venturesome and Beverley Publications or whatever you call yourself. The market just won't stand it. It's tight enough now with Gross and Venturesome fighting each other. There isn't room for a third firm to get in and make a profit, not to speak of upping salaries. So how are you going to do it?"

"Smart", said Beverley in apparent admiration. "Keen. Hard. Bright. Got something in the upper storey. I like it, Davy boy, I like that attitude. You're a thinker. Now let me tell you something. When Jake Beverley does something he does it right, understand. He doesn't make mistakes. Money troubles you just leave to Jake. Look here." He drew a gold-edged wallet from a pocket that seemed uncomfortably full of wallets and cigar and cigarette cases, and flung it on the table. It was bulging with five-pound notes. "You worry your head about whatever it is you do, leave the cashola to Jake, agree?"

"Are you making a firm offer?"

"Not yet." The three-ringed hand waved in the air. "This is a friendly chat inside these four walls."

With an obstinacy I vaguely recognised as foolish I said, "I still don't understand it. What's in it for you?"

Charles Peers tapped one of his science-fiction Calders so that it spun round giving a view of moons and stars successively. "Do you have to see that, Dave?"

"I'm curious, that's all."

Beverley got up and stuck out his stomach at me in a manner obscurely threatening. "Curiosity killed the cat. There are some people shouldn't be too curious. Bad for the health."

"What do you mean?"

Charles Peers began to say something, but Beverley's thick voice wore him down. "People in glass-houses is what I mean. Which is where you are from what I hear. Not that I listen to gossip but there are some things you can't miss." Mary Speed patted a cushion, her husband looked at the floor, Charles Peers set in motion two or three more revolving suns and moons. Beverley twinkled again, his stomach drawn in. "Bad enemy but good friend, that's what they call Jake Beverley. I want to be a friend to you, Davy, if you'll let me. I want to be a friend to everybody. It's when people won't let you be friendly, when they won't be square with you, that it gets me down. You all be square with Jake Beverley and he'll be square with you. And remember, it's the man who sticks his neck out who catches it where the chicken caught the chopper." His stubby fingers picked up the gold-edged wallet and tucked it carefully back in his breast pocket, then he waddled round the room shaking hands. Charles Peers hurried to the door and opened it. Standing at the window I saw Peers stand talking with Beverley a moment in front of the car, while a chauffeur held the door open. Then Beverley shook hands with Peers – he was a great man for shaking hands – and rolled into the car. It might not be gold-plated, but it was a Rolls Royce.

"Quite a character", Mary said when Charles came up again. "How did you meet him, Charles?"

"I've known him quite a while, off and on", Charles said vaguely. "He's like something from another world, don't you think? Rather refreshing."

"Most refreshing", his wife echoed.

"You didn't think so, Dave." Charles poured me another drink. "He's a financier you know, pretty shrewd behind all those stomachs and chins. If he's interested in starting another multiple book show I'd say there must be something in it." He seemed to be choosing his words carefully.

My head was still full of cottonwool. I felt depressed and quarrelsome. "He may be the cat's whiskers. But you know as well as I do that what I said was true. There's no room for a third firm in the business."

O'Kelly blew a smoke ring. "Why don't you let him worry about that? After all, you've got other things on your mind, isn't that so?"

"What things?"

Something about the way I said it must have taken him aback.

"I didn't mean – " He stopped, and tried again. "Mary said you'd been appointed editor of this new magazine. I should have thought getting it going would be enough worry for any three people."

I got up a little unsteadily. "I ought to be going." My headache was back in full force.

Charles came downstairs with me. "Sure you feel all right, Dave?"

Again I saw, more vividly this time, the scene in court. *Nervous and unsettled...tried to pick a quarrel with someone who came round to have a drink, man he'd never met before...obviously under great emotional strain...*

"Perfectly all right."

"Don't take all this too seriously, Beverley, I mean. I daresay nothing will come of it."

I waved to a taxi. From inside it I saw Charles' face glimmering in lamplight. I could see nothing behind the pebbled eyes, but the face showed a look of friendly concern. Then the taxi moved, and he was gone.

Chapter Twenty-Eight

I walked up to the flat, took out my key and then noticed the streak of light under the door. I wondered if I had left the light on, but in fact knew that I had not. Foolishly I looked at the Yale key in my hand, at the locked door, back at the key.

What does one do, I asked myself, in such a case? I thought quite wildly of ringing the bell – *that* would give him a shock. I had suddenly an overwhelming conviction that the visitor, whoever it was, held the solution to the mysteries that oppressed me, my failure in the election, Willie's death, and the obscure connection with it of the Kline-Ross case. I felt also that if I did not immediately open the door I should be failing in some urgent duty. I put the key in the lock and, with no special precaution to keep silent, opened the door.

The light was on in the hall. There was no light in the living-room. The bedroom door was closed. I flung it open. Rose was in bed, eating chocolates and reading *Vogue*. She had on a blue night-dress. Her neck and arms were very white. She put down the copy of *Vogue* and said hallo.

"Rose."

"You sound disappointed. Were you expecting someone else?"

"I don't know. I saw the light and I had a feeling – I don't know." I passed a hand over my face. I felt a spurt of anger at the sight of her sitting up so calmly in bed. "To what do I owe the pleasure?"

She said sharply, "Don't talk like that or there won't be any pleasure. For anybody."

"Couldn't you bear the Third Programme any longer? I don't blame you."

"I came back because I thought you'd want me, I thought we ought to try – " Her lower lip began to quiver.

Why couldn't I say I was delighted to see her back? I tried. "Rose, I didn't mean that crack. Thank you for coming back." I walked over to the bed and took her in my arms. The whiteness of her arms and neck was softly yielding. "Oh, Rose", I said over and over. "Oh, Rose, Rose." My arm knocked the box of chocolates to the floor.

What followed, ecstatic and brief, was better than it had been for a long time and, temporarily at least, a solvent for all troubles. My headache was gone, and my head cleared of cottonwool as if by magic. I lay on the bed by her side, drained of fear and excitement, looking at my legs, one shorter than the other. "I dreamt that you had come back. You were wearing your old red raincoat. But I got the sheet wound round my legs and it turned into a nightmare."

She put her hand on mine. "The Inspector came to see me today. He told me about this woman Christy, and the hotel. Why didn't you tell me that, Dave?"

"I don't know."

"Before that I'd told him the tale you'd given me, about going to the cinema and falling asleep. You should have told me the truth, Dave, you should trust me. You really were with this Christy woman, that's true, isn't it?"

"Of course it is. She looked like you – at least I thought so."

"And did you – "

"No."

"Even if you did you'd say that, wouldn't you? Don't you see it doesn't matter, I don't mind."

"It's perfectly true. I didn't. At least I can't remember." She sighed. I raised myself on one elbow. The respite, a matter of minutes, was over. "Rose, did you come here earlier today, before six o'clock?"

"You're quite sure."

She patted my hand impatiently. "It's not the sort of thing you make a mistake about. Why?"

I told her about the shirts and the missing cigarette lighter. She didn't seem much impressed. I could see that I hadn't any way of making her feel my own conviction that someone else had entered the flat, and if I couldn't convince Rose who knew my fussiness about putting away my own laundry, what chance was there of convincing Inspector Crambo? Exactly none at all. She asked where I'd been that evening and I told her about going to the Peers' flat, about Beverley, about the queer atmosphere there. Again she seemed to think I was probably imagining things.

"Honestly, Dave, I can't see anything odd about it. This man Beverley has money to burn, he wants to get into the multiple book business, and he's buying his way in. What more is there to it?"

"I don't know. But there was something."

"You'd better forget all that and concentrate on your Christy woman. She can't have vanished into thin air."

I made no reply. I was thinking about Willie Strayte, and wondering how best I could ask questions about him. "What did you talk about with Willie? I don't mean on that last night, I mean at any time."

She took her hand off mine. "Why?"

"It might be helpful to know."

"Tell you the truth, Dave, we didn't talk very much at all. I didn't like him much, even, and I don't think he liked me. He certainly didn't trust me. That wasn't our relationship."

"Then what – "

"Don't ask too many questions, or you'll get hurt. He had his fascination, Willie, and for me there was never any more to it than that. AS for him, well, he got a kick out of knowing that I was your wife. Do you want me to go on?"

"Didn't you ever meet any of his friends?"

"Not if he could help it. There was a sort of artist named Bentz we met in a pub once, and an old friend of Willie's named Jack Paulet that we met once or twice. But they never said anything that would be any use to you, nothing at all. Willie was as close as an oyster. Once when I went round to his flat a man named Greener was there, but Willie soon got rid of him."

It took a few seconds for the name to penetrate. When it did I sat up in bed, and winced because my leg hurt. "Greener? What sort of man was he, what age?"

"Quite old. In his seventies I suppose, grizzled, nothing very remarkable about him. Had a bad heart, I remember, didn't like walking up and down stairs."

"Where did he come from, do you know that?"

"I don't know. Yes I do, I remember now. He was a South African, over here on a visit. He knew some people over there who were acquaintances of Willie's, and I think they gave him an introduction." She said slowly, "It's coming back to me now. I only saw him for ten minutes. He'd called for Willie at the office and they'd come round to the flat. Willie made an arrangement to meet him for dinner the following night."

"How long ago was this?"

"About three weeks, perhaps a little more."

That fitted the time when Willie showed interest in the Kline-Ross file. "What was Greener's address in London?"

"I don't know. Yes I do, it was some hotel – Greener asked Willie to get in touch with him there if he wanted him. I think I can remember it – Burlington, Berwick, it began with B – Berriton, that's it, the Berriton Hotel. But what is all this?"

"I'll tell you in a minute. After Greener had gone did Willie seem excited or preoccupied?"

She considered. "Yes, I think he did, though he was always proud of not showing his feelings. I wouldn't like to swear to it.

But I've told you that he was excited about something for a few days before he died, and this might have been the start of it." She said again, "But what does it all *mean?*"

I told her about the disappearance of the Kline-Ross file, about the papers I'd got hold of and the account of the trial in which Greener had been the principal witness, about my telephone call to Jerry Eager which convinced me that I was on the right line, and about my conclusion that Willie Strayte had discovered the identity of Alec Ross. What she had told me now provided one of the links I'd been looking for, the link between Willie Strayte and South Africa. This time she did seem impressed.

I got off the bed and began to walk about the room. "The fact that Greener called for Willie at the office, you see the importance of that."

"Not really. Why is it important?"

"It explains where Greener saw Alec Ross. The way I work it out is something like this. Greener calls to see Willie at the office and X, whoever he is, comes in to talk. He stays for a few minutes, perhaps he's introduced to Greener, more probably not. Anyway, Greener recognises him as Alec Ross who should be serving a prison sentence in South Africa. You and I know that Willie wouldn't have left it at that, he'd have gone on asking questions until he discovered what it was all about. I don't suppose Greener considered telling the authorities – after all, the case took place a good many years ago. But Willie would have pursued it, after smelling out something that might be useful to himself – and finding out that by a stroke of luck we had a file on the case in the office."

"And this X of yours", she said slowly, "must have been one of the five who voted on the editorial appointment for the magazine. Which of them?"

"As far as I can work out it must be Bill Rogers."

"Bill Rogers? That loudmouth." She shook her head. "If that's where your reasoning leads you, I should say there's something wrong with the reasoning."

I said with more confidence than I felt, "Then it's George Pacey or Charles Peers."

Rose lighted a cigarette. "You're putting too much weight on that election. I think some of them just said they'd vote for you and then voted for Willie."

"No. It wasn't like that. You didn't hear George tell me that the election was in the bag that morning. He meant what he said or else he's a hell of a good actor." While I had been talking I had been looking in the telephone book, and now I dialled a number.

"Hallo", I said. "Berriton Hotel? A Mr Greener, Mr David Greener, was staying with you a week or two back. Is he still at the hotel? Oh yes, I see. By air? Did he leave a forwarding address? Thank you." I put down the receiver. "Greener went back to South Africa ten days ago by air. His address is 1375 South Avenue, Cape Town. Let's draft a judicious cable to him asking questions about Alec Ross, and see where that gets us."

"Dave." I was busy with my pencil. "Dave. Are you sure you've told me the truth about all this? Because you can, you know, you can tell me the whole truth."

I put down the pencil. "I'm damned. What do I have to say to convince you? Are you another of those who talks on my side and acts the other way?"

"I'm on your side, don't ever doubt that. I'll always be on your side, Dave, if you'll let me." She jumped out of bed. "I'm hungry. Shall I make some sandwiches?"

"I'm hungry too. But not for sandwiches."

I didn't finish writing the cable, and that night there were no nightmares.

Chapter Twenty-Nine

In the morning I sent off the cable on the way to the office. I asked Greener to let me know if he had identified a man named Alec Ross to the late Willie Strayte. I said it was vitally important without explaining why, and signed myself David Nelson, Gross Enterprises. I kept the cable as short as I could, but even so it cost quite a lot of money. I realised that what I should have done according to routine was tell my ideas to the police and let them send the cable, but somehow I didn't feel any conviction that they would pursue it. Rightly or wrongly, it seemed to me that Inspector Crambo wasn't on my side.

Whether or not he was on my side, he was on my tail. I found him sitting in a chair in my room, manicuring his nails. Today he was wearing a different pin-stripe suit, brown in colour, but he was as brisk as ever. "Hallo there. Bright and early, Mr Nelson. It's the early bird that catches the worm, they tell me."

On this particular morning I felt equal to Crambo. "And since you're undoubtedly the early bird, Inspector, what does that make me?"

He showed a large number of his fine teeth in a hearty laugh. "Very good, oh very good indeed. You're much too keen for me, Mr Nelson. I didn't mean it that way at all. Just dropped in to give you the latest news. We seem to have identified your Christy."

"You've found her?"

"I didn't say that. No, we've identified her in the sense that she seems to fit in pretty well to your description, is known in the Gongora Street area and is thought to have patronised the Gongora Residential a good deal. Her name's Christy Freeman. Used to be called by other names too, sometimes, Chris or Chrissie Hallett, did you know that?"

"I told you that I met her for the first and only time that evening."

"So you did. Well, this Christy exists – if she is your Christy. But we haven't yet found anybody who knows where she lives, or anyone who saw her go into the Gongora that night – or come out of it. And she hasn't been seen round her usual haunts in the last few days."

"I put in some time looking for my Christy myself", I said. "Somebody mentioned the name of Christy Freeman. Isn't it unusual to have difficulty in finding out where she lives?"

I offered him a cigarette and lit one myself I looked on the desk for my lighter, but it wasn't there. Crambo produced a match, lit up and puffed reflectively before answering me.

"Not very. There are two or three different sorts of prostitute outside the really high-grade ones. One sort operates from home through massage advertisements and that sort of thing. They never go on the streets at all. Another sort goes on the streets and takes men back to their flats. They're what most people think of as the only kind, but they're wrong. And a third group has an arrangement with two or three hotels so that they can take men to them. Then they go back at night to their perfectly respectable suburban homes. That's the group this Christy Freeman probably belonged to, from what you tell me about the photograph of her son and so on. There's no doubt she had a connection with the Gongora Residential." Crambo stopped and looked at me as if expecting something like a small round of applause. I was not inclined to give it to him.

"Then that shows the little man – what was his name, Morgan – was lying when he said he'd never seen her."

"Oh, he'd lie if there was any need to, never doubted that." Crambo looked at the ash on his cigarette, then airily tapped it on the carpet. "The question is did he need to, if you take me. Putting it man to man, what I mean is this. Morgan lied about never having heard of this Christy woman, or seen her. Whether he lied about not seeing her on Monday night is another thing."

"Hadn't you better get after him and ask a few questions? He's lied about not knowing her and he lied about that evening, you've got my word for that."

"Good idea." Crambo sounded quite enthusiastic. "Only one difficulty in the way. Morgan's disappeared."

"Morgan", I said in surprise.

"Vamoosed, skedaddled, hooked it. A regular vanishing trick, isn't it, the whole case? First you meet this Christy and she disappears, then this Morgan sees you – or doesn't see you – at the hotel and he disappears too. Quite a puzzle. I had to rub my eyes to make sure you were here this morning." Crambo laughed heartily as though he had said something funny.

"If Morgan's gone, doesn't that prove my story's true?"

He put it rather differently. "Certainly is convenient for you. Quite discredits him, doesn't it? But jumping to conclusions just lands you in the mud. Morgan had a record – he'd been inside a couple of times, once for receiving, the other time for helping to run a disorderly house. A man like that doesn't like being questioned by us, even when he's in the clear and only has to stick to his story. And when it's a matter of a murder case, that really sends shivers up his spine. So he ducks out. That's the simplest explanation, and very likely the true one."

I said boldly. "There's another. Somebody's trying to plant this thing on me. Christy Freeman disappeared because she could have given me an alibi, and now Morgan's disappeared because they were afraid he wouldn't stick to his story under pressure."

Pretending surprise like a corny actor, Crambo slapped his knee. "*That's* an idea now. And who could this enemy be? Who knew about you going to the Gongora Hotel with this Christy woman?" I was silent. Abandoning his play-acting suddenly and looking almost grim, Crambo said: "That's a question we've asked ourselves in considering this idea of yours. And we haven't been able to answer it. Can *you* answer it?"

I said reluctantly, "No." It was on the tip of my tongue to tell him about the visitor to my flat, but I didn't do it. If Crambo found it hard to believe my story about going to the hotel he certainly wouldn't accept this tale about a visitor to the flat who had taken nothing except possibly a cigarette lighter. Lamely I said, "That's part of the puzzle too."

"Almost the biggest part." Crambo looked admiringly at the knife-edge crease in his trousers and said casually, "What's all this about South Africa?"

I hesitated, wondering how much to tell him, how much he would believe. Then I told him the whole trail that began with Miss Richards coming in and asking me for the Kline-Ross file, went on to the material I'd obtained through Sandy Donovan, continued with the confirmation I'd got from Jerry Eager that Willie had been interested in the legal aspect of the case, and finished up with the clincher about David Greener.

I'll do Crambo the justice to say that he listened keenly enough to the story, his light eyes staring hard at me all the time, one highly polished brown shoe waving elegantly in the air every so often. "Ingenious", he said when I'd finished, "Right down clever. But what have you got in the way of facts? Nothing that can't be explained quite easily by saying that Strayte found something in this case that might be used as a story for this new magazine of yours. You don't agree? Just see how naturally it goes. Strayte meets Greener, and Greener knows Strayte's connected with the Crime section of your firm. It would be quite natural for him to say 'Ever heard of the Kline-Ross case, I was chief witness in it' or something like that. Greener tells the story, Strayte thinks there might be something in it. Naturally enough he gets hold of a file on the case. Naturally enough he rings up this solicitor of yours to find out the legal position. Trouble with you literary fellows is you're too ingenious. I respect it, mind you, I admire it, but – "

"What happened to the file? You haven't explained that?"

He flashed his teeth at me. "A real detective can never explain everything. There are always loose ends. The file will probably turn up. And mind you, I could be wrong. There are times when the ingenious solution is the right one. And believe me it's a real education for an ordinary man like me to discuss these things with you. You might say it makes me think."

I ignored that. "We shall know what's right when I get the reply to that cable."

"Perhaps." He stood up, a medium-sized man in a brown suit, the kind of man you wouldn't look at twice in the street. "Thank you for giving me so much of your time."

"How did you know I was interested in South Africa?"

"We like to know what's going on", he said vaguely. It seemed to me that his mind was on something else. Presently he said – and it seemed to me that he was choosing his words with care – "You've based this theory on the idea that Strayte jockeyed you out of the editorship on the voting. There could be another explanation of that, you know."

"What do you mean?"

He didn't answer but with his hand on the door-knob went on talking. "In my experience cases are almost always solved by the checking and re-checking that I talked to you about the other day. We often know the name of a murderer a long time before we arrest him. The rope is already hanging over his shoulders, you might say, but so lightly that he can't feel it. Every check we make on every minor point draws it just an inch tighter. When he first feels it he thinks he can easily slip his head out of such a slack noose, so easily that he doesn't try. Later on he does try, but by then it's too late. He manufactures evidence, he tries to hide evidence, he finds a new story or constructs an alibi. Useless, all of it. Every move and wriggle he makes now simply narrows the circle of rope another inch or two, because the more stories he invents the more inconsistencies there will be in them. At last he really feels the touch of rope round his neck and then – "

"And then?"

"The case is finished." He smiled at me. "I don't think the solution to this case is going to come in a cable from South Africa. I think it's in an answer to this question: Is there anybody, anybody at all, who hates you enough to try and plant this murder on you? Is there anybody at all who could have arranged the disappearance of your Christy?"

I shook my head helplessly. "I don't know."

"Then you'd better find out. And quickly."

Chapter Thirty

That morning Solly Birkett brought in his ideas for the six months' run of the crime cartoon strip. The chief character, Rosemary, was a girl who won a beauty contest which guaranteed her a film part and a six months' stage engagement. The contest had been fixed in advance, of course, and Rosemary achieved her film part (which turned out to be third hoofer from the left in a musical comedy) by means of the casting director's sofa. The star took a fancy to her and introduced her to a drug-taking theatrical group. Then she tried the stage engagement which turned out to be in South America, where she was expected to act as hostess to a variety of lascivious natives. In the end a clean-jawed Errol Flynn type of visiting English sea-dog saved her from a fate worse than death – she had suffered this fate several times already but this time the male incumbent was a Negro – and took her back to the Old Country and wedding bells. Even from Solly's rough sketches I could see that this cartoon story would be a winner.

"Good, Solly. I like it." But there was a thing that bothered me. "Why did you call her Rosemary? I thought Hep mentioned Nellie."

"I know he did but, Dave, we can't use a name like that. Little Nellie's a dirty joke in itself you know, little Nellie and her great big belly."

"But why pick on Rosemary?"

"Sounded a good English peaches and cream lady-in-distress name, that's all. What's wrong with it?"

"Just that my wife's name is Rose, that's all."

"But what the hell, Dave." Solly began to laugh, stopped as he saw my face. "Of course, if that's the way you feel about it."

"It is the way I feel about it."

"Let's change it then. Nothing personal intended, Dave, you know that." Solly had tight dark curls, a thin hooked nose and a hard, tight little face. "Call her Pamela, that's a pretty juicy name. All right?"

"Fine. And that Negro at the end, I don't know about him."

"Don't know about him? Why, he's part of the moral warning in the story. If you don't want your little Pamela laid by Negroes, Mrs Fitzlangley, keep her away from those beauty contests."

"Substitute Jew for Negro, Solly, and would you still think it was funny?"

Solly's tight little face looked tighter than usual. "Pardon me, but I left my principles at home today along with my winter undies. I thought the weather was too fine for them."

"No kidding, Solly, this is playing with something dangerous. And dangerous for you especially, I'm telling you."

Solly spread out his hands. "You're telling me? Is it news, that? I'm a Hackney Jew, Dave. At school they called us Ikeymoes and Jewboys, we organised gangs to fight them and they had bigger gangs to fight us and catch us when we were out alone. In the war I never got above sergeant's rank because of the shape of my nose. There was another sergeant who wouldn't sit at table with me because he said he didn't like Jew smell. You think you can tell me anything about what people are like, Dave? You think I'm going to blush at calling a Negro a dirty nigger, you got another think coming. You want to wake up yourself, Dave, and take a look around you, take a look in the mirror too maybe. What else did you put me on this job for but because I'm a Jew?"

I hadn't any answer. "Let's not argue, Solly. We'll leave him a dirty nigger." The door opened and Rose came in. "Nothing personal intended."

"And no offence taken. Hallo there, Mrs Nelson. You want to be careful of Dave today, he's just been giving me a lesson in the ethics of writing strip cartoons."

Rose smiled vaguely as though she did not hear what he said. Her face was very pale. When Solly had closed the door behind him I said, "Look what the cat's brought in? Or should I say to what do I owe the honour of this unexpected visit?" For it was a fact that Rose hardly ever came to the office.

She was wearing a plain black suit with a little silver ornament on the shoulder, and I saw that her pallor was partly due to the fact that she had on almost no make-up. Now she snapped open a small cylindrical black bag and took from it a piece of paper which she handed to me. The piece of paper had a name and address typed on it. I read: *Christy Freeman, 17g Callaway Street, W2.*

"I found it in the chest of drawers this morning," Rose said in a matter of fact way. "Under some stockings."

I stared at it unbelievingly. "This must have been put there when they broke into the flat."

"I thought you'd say that." She didn't sound enthusiastic.

"What else do you suppose? Do you think I put it there myself?"

"I don't think anything. I don't know what I think, I thought you'd better see it, that's all."

I stood up and patted her on the shoulder. Then I stared at the typed address as though it ought to tell me something. With a sort of reluctance I couldn't understand I said, "We'd better go out and have a look at this place. The Inspector came in this morning and said the whole case might be cleared up if we could find Christy Freeman." That wasn't exactly what he had said, but it seemed near enough.

Chapter Thirty-One

"This is it." The cab-driver stopped and we got out. Callaway Street was in the network of dingy streets at the back of Praed Street and Paddington Station. Number seventeen presented a decayed Victorian front and a gaping entrance hall. Bell pushes outside said *a* Schwartz, *b* Mariakis, *c* Jones, *d* Clancy, *e* Ghoty, *f* Bannerjee, *g* Freeman. The name Freeman was faded. I pressed the bell and we waited. The day was sunny, but with a nipping wind. Perhaps it was the wind that made Rose shiver.

I moved into the entrance hall. "Now that we're here, let's go a bit further."

She put a hand on my arm. She was trembling. "Dave, I don't like it."

"There's nothing to be afraid of." Inside the hall was an uncarpeted stairway and a door with the letter *a* on it. "Freeman's at the top. Get ready to climb."

She still hung back. "If she doesn't answer what's the good of going up?"

"If you think I'm going back without seeing her front door after coming this far, you're wrong." I began to walk up the stairs, slowly because of my leg, and she followed me reluctantly. Flats *b* and *c* were on the second floor, *d*, *e*, and *f* on the third. Their chocolate-brown doors were shut and no sound came from behind them. The house was silent as if nobody had lived in it for years, the staircase was dark and smelt musty. The staircase narrowed after the third floor, and moved windingly into what must long ago have been the attics or servants' bedrooms. At the top of those winding stairs there was no landing but simply a door, painted light blue in contrast to the prevailing chocolate brown below. I pushed at the door, but it was shut.

Rose was now quite definitely shivering. "Now you've seen it, can we go?"

Above the door was a large skylight. With difficulty I hoisted myself up with my good foot resting on the stair rail and the other one with its great lump of wooden heel resting on a ledge that projected a few inches outside the door. Through the skylight I saw a tiny hall, and beyond it the corner of a room with a chair overturned, and pieces of glass on the floor. I wrapped a handkerchief around my hand, almost slipping down from my position as I did so, and then punched the glass. It broke and fell inwards. Rose gave a brief cry.

I knocked away more glass until there was enough room for me to go through the skylight.

"What's inside?" she asked.

"That's what I'm going to find out." It was awkward to get through but I managed it, cutting my hand only a little on fragments of glass left in the frame. I jumped down inside and felt a brief thrill of pain in my bad foot. Then I opened the front door. Rose hovered on the threshold.

There was a closed door to the left, but I moved towards the living room I had seen through the skylight. It was in a state of great disorder. Ornaments had been swept off the mantelpiece and broken, chairs were overturned, the cloth had been pulled off a table that stood in the middle of the room. A bottle of gin had been knocked to the floor and some of its contents had seeped out over the carpet. Two glasses lay near it, one broken and the other intact. On the floor also lay a photograph frame. Below the shattered glass the face of Christy Freeman's son, which I had seen so many ages ago, looked up at me. By the photograph frame was the black plastic bag that I remembered from the wine bar. Its contents, lipstick, vanity case, powder puff, ballpoint pen, were scattered over the floor.

I saw all these things afterwards. What I saw now was the body of Christy Freeman lying on a divan in one corner of the room. Her face was purple and swollen. She had been dead some time.

I walked quickly over to the window, which overlooked the roofs of the street at the back. I flung the window wide open and leaned out of it, taking in great draughts of air. Rose chose that moment to enter the flat and look in at the door. She screamed.

I jerked my head in from the window. She was standing looking at the body on the divan with her hand in front of her mouth – in what I couldn't help thinking was the traditional position of screen heroines confronted by horrors – and she was screaming quite loudly. I slapped her face, acting in the tradition of the screen hero and she stopped.

"Just pull yourself together and listen. Go out, find a telephone, ring up Inspector Crambo at Scotland Yard. Tell him where we are and what we've found. Then come back here."

"I can't come back. I don't want to see – "

"Very well, then go home."

"Is that the woman, that woman in there?" I nodded. She began to laugh loudly. Between gasps of laughter she said, "You told me she was like me. I know, I know, don't say it, I'm hysterical. Better when I'm in the air. Don't worry, I'll telephone."

I watched her go down the stairs with some misgiving. Then I opened the door to the left, which led to a bathroom and kitchenette. The door to the bedroom led through the living-room. Nothing in any of these rooms seemed to have been much disturbed.

My hand was bleeding slightly from the cuts made when I climbed through the skylight. I went out to the bathroom, washed my hand and dried it on a towel. I went back and looked at Christy Freeman, forcing myself to go fairly close to her.

There was no sign of blood, but I could see discolorations on her throat. While I was kneeling by her side my eye caught the glint of some bright object under the divan.

I lay flat, got out the object, took it into the bedroom and sat staring at it. It was my own silver cigarette lighter. I snapped it open and the thing lighted. I read the inscription: *D From R. Lighting Up Time.*

Chapter Thirty-Two

I was still sitting in the bedroom when Crambo arrived rather more than half an hour later, accompanied by a small army of policemen, some photographers, others fingerprint men, others still more general busybodies. I had expected that he would talk to me at once, but he simply acknowledged my presence with a curt nod and then busied himself with what I should have thought was the routine process of having the room and the body photographed from twenty different angles. Occasionally he called out questions to me, asking what I'd touched in the room, whether I'd moved anything, whether Rose had come into the room and so on. I answered the questions without saying anything about the cigarette lighter. The rubber band was back again inside my forehead, expanding and contracting as though it belonged to a catapult. I was impressed against my will by the frantic busyness of the police operations and by what seemed to be Crambo's efficiency. He would have made a good Executive Editor for us.

A doctor arrived to look at the body. Crambo came into the bedroom where I was sitting, and closed the door between bedroom and living-room. His usual air of jauntiness had disappeared. I remembered my first comparison of him with a man who was selling insurance, and thought that he looked now like an insurance salesman who has just lost a big contract to a rival. That is to say, he was trying to look grim and managed only to seem peevish.

He stared hard at me and then spoke. "Let's have it. I got some sort of story from your wife on the telephone. She said she was going home. I shall want to talk to her again later, but I'll take your story now. Sergeant Matheson." A square-jawed man came in, sat on a pink-frilled laundry basket and took out a notebook. Crambo sat down in a pink basket-weave chair and I remained on the bed.

I handed him the typed note and told him about Rose finding it. I told him also of my belief that my flat had been entered.

"Why didn't you say that this morning?"

"What would have been the use? It was all an impression of mine based on the fact that the wrong shirt was on top of the pile in the drawer. You'd have laughed at me."

"I'm not laughing now. Did you look in the drawer where your wife found this slip of paper?"

"I may have opened it. I didn't look closely inside. I was looking for things that might have been taken away, not things that had been planted in the flat."

"Did you find anything had been taken?"

"I wasn't sure about my cigarette lighter. I thought I might have left it at the office."

The Sergeant wrote it all down. "Anything else?"

"I couldn't see anything else."

"Had you left the lighter at the office?"

"No. I found it under the divan in there. Here it is." I took the lighter out of my pocket and handed it to him.

He stared at the lighter and he stared at me. "I'll be damned", he said softly. "You're telling me that you found this lighter underneath the divan where her body's lying now."

"Yes."

"And you expect me to believe that somebody – this enemy of yours – killed Christy Freeman, got into your flat, took the lighter and put it under the body. That's what you expect me to believe."

I remembered what Jack Dimmock had said to me. "I don't know what you'll believe. It's the truth and it's the only story I've got and they say if you tell the truth it can't hurt you."

"But why tell me about it at all? You picked up the lighter and put it in your pocket. Why not leave it at that, why make the police a present of something which, if we don't believe your story, is a powerful argument against you?"

Behind the rubber band, expanding and contracting, infinitely flexible, I could feel the rumour of a headache. "I've reached a point where I just don't know what's happening to me. There may be other things of mine planted in this flat. The truth may look bad, but lies would be worse."

"Shall I tell you the commonsense explanation of the way you've acted? Strayte died on Monday night. You killed Christy Freeman, perhaps the same night, probably on Tuesday. She was strangled, you know that I expect. There was a cord round her neck, though you can hardly see it now for swollen flesh."

"I guessed she'd been strangled."

"Then yesterday you missed your cigarette lighter – or perhaps it wasn't the lighter at all, it may have been something else altogether. Whatever it was, you realised that you must get it. You didn't dare to come here alone because of the chance that you might be seen, so you put that address where you knew your wife was certain to find it. You discovered the body together, then you sent her off to telephone me and retrieved whatever it was you'd left here. As a final piece of ingenuity, a double bluff to baffle the stupid detective they call Dumb Crambo you actually admit that your lighter was here, and suggest that it has been planted. Very clever." Crambo's lower lip was petulantly outthrust, his face was gloomy. He had forgotten to pull up the knees of his trousers.

"You don't really believe that?"

"Why shouldn't I believe it?" Somebody knocked on the door and the sergeant went over to it. He came across and whispered to Crambo, who got up and went out. The sergeant sat down again on the laundry basket and immediately became busy with his notebook. I got up and walked about the room. I passed him as I walked, and glanced across to see what he was writing. In fact he was not writing, but making a small, realistic drawing of a man hanging on a gallows. He did not look up.

When Crambo returned he had recovered something of his usual bounce. "Christy Freeman was almost certainly killed on Tuesday, not before Tuesday evening anyway. Does that mean anything to you?" I shook my head. "Don't say I'm not helping you with information. Now, you were going to tell me why I shouldn't believe that you'd arranged to discover the body yourself."

I spoke with an assurance I didn't feel. "Don't forget I've written and supervised a lot of detective stories. Give me credit for a bit of sense. You said I'd been very clever, but if I'd behaved in the way you suggest I should need my head examining." Sergeant Matheson looked up from his notebook – was he really making notes, I wondered, or still drawing that man on the gallows? – with a hard smile. "If I'd really killed Christy Freeman and left something here, do you suppose I couldn't have found half a dozen ways of getting it? Watching the flats to make sure nobody was in and then nipping quickly up the stairs, for instance? Or even disguising myself a bit and coming up as a gas-meter reader or something, using a glass cutter on the skylight instead of my fist wrapped in a handkerchief. You can tell when you walk up the stairs that this is a house where the tenants mostly let each other alone. I believe Christy Freeman could have stayed here for a fortnight and nobody would have bothered about her. I had only to take a bit of care, and the chance of discovery was very slight. But what do I do instead according to you? I put a note in a drawer with her address on it, just to show the police that I knew where she was all the time. I bring my wife along as a witness. And having got back whatever it was I'm supposed to have left here I decide just for fun to make you suspicious by telling you all about it. Fine murderer I am, I must say. If one of our story writers made a murderer act like that he'd get his dictabook back with a few rude remarks about sticking to the laws of probability, I can tell you."

"Would he really?" Crambo seemed interested. "You keep a ruler on your desk to rap them over the knuckles, do you? Metaphorically I mean", he added with a cackle of laughter.

"Not all that often. All the general plot outlines are arranged by a committee of the Section Editor and Executive Editors before the story writer gets to work." There was something the Inspector had said or suggested which, I seemed to think, had a special meaning for me. Behind the headache, which was turning from rumour to reality, I tried to think what it was. "If the plant had worked as it was meant to work somebody would eventually have found Christy Freeman here. Under the divan would have been my lighter, in the drawer at my flat you'd have found her address. That would have made a pretty unanswerable case against me. It was the purest chance that Rose opened that drawer and found the note."

"You fairly baffle me with science." Crambo had pulled up the knees of his trousers now, exposing gaily-patterned brown socks. "I expect you're right. After all, if you chaps who are writing about crime all day don't know about criminal psychology, who does? Ever had your fingerprints taken?"

"No." I remembered now. Crambo had told me that Christy Freeman had been killed almost certainly on Tuesday, not before Tuesday evening, and had asked if that meant anything to me. I had shaken my head, but now I had the feeling that there was some significance about this time. Tuesday evening? On Tuesday evening I had gone down to see Rose. On Wednesday morning I had been appointed editor of the magazine, and at lunchtime had gone to see the barman at the Select wine bar and the registration clerk at the Gongora Hotel. What was there in that?

"Quite an experience", the Inspector said. "Every editor of a crime magazine should know about that kind of thing. Care to try it? Help us to sort out the tangle of prints next door."

"Very well." Crambo stood up. Matheson stood up. I stood up. Matheson opened the door. It seemed that the interview was over. In the sitting-room men were still moving about like ants, dusting and taking photographs. Christy Freeman's body had gone. I put my fingers on the inky pad and then on the sheet they gave me. The marks came out black and clear. Crambo said cheerfully, "Pretty-looking things, aren't they? Funny to think they can hang a man." I thought of the drawing in Matheson's notebook. "Thank you for your co-operation. And instruction almost, you might say."

I walked down the stairs, through the dark entrance hall, out into Callaway street. The day had clouded over now and as I walked along towards Praed Street, trying to remember what should have been important to me about the time of Christy Freeman's death, large drops of rain began to fall.

Chapter Thirty-Three

In the ordinary way I don't suppose any of us ever think of the amount of time that is wasted in our lives. Sleeping, dressing, washing, shaving, waiting for buses and trains and then riding to and from work, standing at traffic lights waiting until they change, waiting to be served in restaurants or in pubs – probably a quarter of our waking lives is spent waiting for something to happen, if you think of it that way. Most of us don't think of it that way, of course, but this afternoon I had a strong and oppressive feeling that I was waiting for something to happen. Or put it another way and say that I felt I ought to be doing something or other which was urgently important for me, but was somehow prevented from doing so.

I went back to the office, and took three sodium amytal tablets, although I'd been told not to take more than one. They seemed to push back the headache to a place inside my head where it didn't bother me. I rang up Rose at home, but could get no reply. When I got no reply from the flat I felt that it was vitally important for me to speak to her. Three times during the afternoon I telephoned the flat and got no reply. That was one thing that worried me. Another was the fact that I had proved to my own satisfaction – though that wasn't really the word – that George Pacey, Bill Rogers or Charles Peers must be the man I was after. I'd promised myself that I would do some research into their backgrounds, and this research hadn't started yet. Here again I felt that time was running short, something decisive was likely to happen soon. With all this going through my head I still tried to keep my mind on Mary Speed's version of the Rouse case, which lay on my desk in dictabook form.

It was impossible to concentrate on the story, but I found myself admiring her fresh, crisp voice and wondering how a smart girl like Mary could have got herself married to a man like O'Kelly, who frankly had impressed me as a large-sized cipher. I found myself thinking about Jake Beverley and Charles Peers, and pulled up with a jerk. There was another dictabook on the desk, a locked room mystery of Harold Paynter's. I put that on too, but couldn't keep my mind on it for more than a couple of minutes, so I took it off again. My impression was that it stank, but I thought I ought to give the thing another chance. I had picked up the telephone receiver to try Rose again when there was a timid knock on the door, and Sandy Donovan's head peered round it.

"I wondered – " he said uneasily. " – But not if you're busy."

I put down the telephone with an inexplicable feeling of relief. "Never too busy to talk to a man with bright ideas."

"It was only – I don't know how to put it – I felt a bit out of things and wondered if you'd got anything for me."

"Out of things ?"

His voice dropped to a kind of schoolboy's mutter, slightly incoherent. "Everyone else working on the magazine – thought I might – that thing you put me on to, Kline-Ross – be able to do something – "

It was his mention of the Kline-Ross case that gave me the idea, a good idea it seemed to my thoroughly confused mind. "Come right in, Sandy, don't prop the door up. I've got something I'd like you to work on, and it's fairly hush-hush. There may be nothing to it, but I'd like to try it out."

His face took on a ludicrous look of dog-like expectation.

"What I've got in mind is running a feature story every so often on what goes on inside the firm, a personal slant. The personalities behind the crime stories you enjoy, you get the line." My voice seemed to be coming from a long way away. Sandy nodded. "Take George Pacey. George is a hell of a good Section Editor, we all know that, but what else is he? All I know, or you or most other people, is that George is a good family man and a nice chap in general, but there must be more to it than that. Somewhere there's a gimmick about George that gives him his particular flair for telling a good crime story from a dud one. What is it, what's his background, what makes him tick? He's been with us for *x* years, what did he do before that? All I know is that he was at Benedict's Grammar School, and I only know that because there's a chap named Jack Mayne in Science Fiction who was at school with him when George was ten years old. You might start with Mayne, find out what happened to George afterwards. Maybe he went to another school, maybe he stopped his schooling at fourteen, maybe he went to a University, maybe he even went abroad. Do some discreet digging and find out."

Sandy looked at me as if he thought I was crazy. "You mean *Crime Magazine* might run an article on George Pacey."

"Could be. May be nothing in it, can't tell until we try it out. It's by trying over a dozen different ideas and chucking out eleven of them that we finally get a good one. Negative and positive, you know." I could hear that I was talking too much.

"If you think all this stuff's important why don't you just ask Mr Pacey?"

I was prepared for that one, or at least I thought I was. "We can't do it that way. Don't you see the essence of the thing is that George himself doesn't know what makes him tick? This will be investigating ourselves from the inside, really taking ourselves apart, don't you see that?"

The look on Sandy's face, mulish, discontented and disbelieving, told me I'd gone too far. He was fairly simple, but he wasn't quite the half-wit I'd been playing him for. "No, I don't see it. Seems to me all you want is for me to find out about

George Pacey's life, act as a sort of spy. I don't know why you want it, but that's the way it seems to me."

A hammer struck in my head, repeating a refrain, *Gone* too far you've *gone* too far *gone* too far you've *gone* too far. I stared at the desk. I could not trust myself to look up at Sandy Donovan's face. "Forget it, Sandy. It was just an idea, perhaps not a very hot one."

The change in Sandy's voice was very noticeable. Usually he could hardly keep out the worshipful note when he talked to me, but something else was in it now, uncertainty and perhaps even suspicion. "It's the thinnest story I've ever heard. Got no meaning to it at all. Don't understand why you should have tried it on me expect because you think I'm a fool."

Under the desk my hands twisted together as though they were creatures with separate identities of their own. "I said to forget it, Sandy. George is a good friend of mine.

"I wouldn't want to keep anything from you. All the business about that case, Kline-Ross, I don't believe it was for the magazine at all. I told the Inspector about it." At that I did look up. Sandy's face was brick red, the freckles standing out on it. He looked both embarrassed and forlorn. "I know you think I'm not much good at the job, but you shouldn't have tried to use me like that. I'm going to have to tell the Inspector about this business too."

The hammer went on in my head, *gone* too far, *gone* too far, oh poor old Dave he's *gone* too far. I said wearily, "You're right about one thing, Sandy, you're no good at the job. George and Willie Strayte both said so, and they were right. You don't belong here. You're fired, and one day you'll bless me for firing you. Check it with George if you like, but he'll only tell you the same thing in different words."

Sandy's face got redder. "I knew you wouldn't like it, but I had to tell you and I don't see why you should take it – "

I stood up and shouted at him. "Get out. Do what you like and tell anybody anything you like, but get out of this office."

When he was outside the room I said aloud, "You're a fool, Dave Nelson." Then I put my head on the desk and after a moment felt the tears, warm and soothing, flowing out of my eyes.

Chapter Thirty-Four

As I was leaving I met Charles Peers in the entrance hall. He looked at me for a moment over his glasses as if he didn't know me, and then spoke. "What are you doing this evening? There's an interesting concert of Tibetan music on at Wigmore Hall if you – "

"I'm busy."

"I thought you might be." I didn't know how to take him, whether it was a joke or not. "I shouldn't take that business last night too seriously."

"Last night?"

"Jake Beverley. He doesn't mean everything he says."

"I hadn't thought much about it", I said quite honestly.

"He may seem a rough diamond but he's really rather a good chap." Charles spoke the words with unction, and in his mouth they seemed more than usually ridiculous. "One of the best."

Depressed as I felt I almost raised a laugh at this. "Don't overdo it, Charles."

"I mean it. And I happen to know he thinks very highly of you", he added, if possible more solemnly still. "Think it over." With that he left me wondering, as I had often wondered before, whether he was what he seemed to be – an arty boy who had strayed into our kind of book racket – or whether he was really a shrewd operator who was putting on an act about Tibetan music and Indian dances and psychoanalysis and that sort of stuff. I never had made up my mind about that, and probably I never should.

I had tried the flat a couple of more times before leaving the office, but had got no reply. On an impulse I had also tried Marian's place at Croydon, but I got no reply from there either. Wherever Rose was she wasn't at home, and there seemed no point in going home. I drifted into the Rubicon Club, sat down at one of the stools and ordered a whisky. It seemed a long time, though in fact it was only four days, that I'd been in here drinking with Mary Speed and Bill Rogers, and thinking that my worst misfortune was to have been tricked out of a magazine editorship. The place was empty except for a couple of people I didn't know, and I sat with the whisky in front of me and thought about all my problems.

I wondered where Rose was and what the Inspector really thought of me and what Sandy Donovan would tell him, and what to do about Bill Rogers. Then my thoughts from being vague were pinpointed on Rose, and from being cloudy became suddenly clear. At the back of my mind I suppose there had been the thought of Rose and Willie Strayte, always, ever since I had learned about them. I had balked at thinking about their relationship, but now it seemed to me that discovery of this relationship had been the basis for everything I'd done. And it occurred to me with a *clang* of surprise, the clang mute but thunderous in my head, how directly all my troubles were connected with Rose. She has an affair with Willie, he is murdered – and at once I'm the chief suspect. Rose is the guilty party in the affair, putting it in police court language, but it's Rose who gets everybody's sympathy. Then Rose comes back to me, saying let's try again and everything's going to be all right from now on or some such words, Rose finds the note so that I discover Christy Freeman's body and land my two feet deeper in the mess. Having done this Rose, who loves me, skips off again. In the role of prosecuting counsel I asked: haven't I made out a case for this Rose having some deliberate intention of causing the prisoner's downfall? In the part of jury I nodded agreement and ordered another whisky. As I was stretching out my hand to it another hand swooped and took the drink, a husky voice said: "Thanks, stranger."

Sonia Rogers, all six feet of her, stood with my glass of whisky in her hand, smiling at me. She was a blonde hearty woman in her late thirties or early forties, a gigantic English rose slightly overblown. She still had overwhelming vitality, good teeth and a lot of hair, but her hips had thickened and she was developing a noticeable jowl. The trouble about Sonia was that she didn't know her age and she went on doing things, like taking my drink away, that might have seemed terribly gay if she'd been fifteen years younger.

However, sight of Sonia reminded me that I might be able to do some digging into Bill's past, so I stifled my irritation and ordered another drink.

"That son of a bitch husband of mine, do you know what he's done to me? Just stood me up beautifully, that's all. All the week we've arranged he should keep tonight free as a kind of anniversary. We meet here straight after he leaves that temple of vice you call a publishing company, we tank up a little, we go out to dinner, we dance, we go home. What you might call a celebration, though as a celebration it's quiet, wouldn't you say?"

"No celebration would be quiet with you around, Sonia. What's it in aid of?"

"The day we fixed ourselves up with a ball and chain, though why we did it I don't know."

"What's that?"

"Marriage. I'm talking about, haven't you heard the word, I'll spell it out for you, B, E, D. And believe me if I'd known then what I know now – " She didn't complete the sentence but threw back her head and laughed, revealing a well-shaped but slightly sagging white throat.

"Congratulations anyway. Tank up." I rolled my head around, to convince myself that my headache had in fact gone.

"What are you doing?"

"Just shaking those old blue devils out of my head."

"Is that so? This one's on me." She ordered two double whiskies and said with some ferocity, "If you think I'm going to tell you how old I am, Dave Nelson, you're wrong. I've fixed my age at thirty-two, and in my year there are no birthdays."

"You could call it thirty and still look on the right side of it", I lied gallantly. "And at that you and Bill could easily have been married ten years. Is that what it is, ten years?"

She put a hand on mine. Her hand was like everything else about Sonia, large, fleshy and powerful. "I like you, Dave, do you know that? I've always liked you. I've always stood up for you, I won't hear anything against you. He's conceited, they tell me, he's a cold fish, with him it's number one first and the rest nowhere. No, no, I tell 'em, you don't know him, Dave's not like that, he's just a boy at heart."

"It's good to know I've got a friend. Who says all these nice things about me?"

"Just people. People can be lousy. I know, I've been through it. But I'm for you, I've always been for you, Dave." I couldn't make out whether she'd been drinking before she met me, or whether it was just Sonia's natural exuberance.

"What people?"

She shook her head vigorously and took her hand off mine. "I'm no scandalmonger. Wild horses wouldn't drag any more from me." I should have felt a lot of sympathy for any wild horse unwise enough to try to drag Sonia around. "But I was telling you how this bastard husband of mine broke our date. Suddenly rings up this afternoon, says he's got an important interview, may be a little late, I'm to come and wait here for him. What do you think about that, don't you call it cool?"

"I do that. Especially on your silver wedding anniversary."

"Who said anything about a silver wedding?"

"Didn't you say you'd been married ten years? I thought that was silver."

"I didn't say anything about how long it was, Dave Nelson, and anyway ten years isn't silver."

"My mistake."

"Your mistake, I'll say it's your mistake, and it's not the only mistake you've made. Shall I tell you something about yourself? You don't know women, Dave."

"Who does?"

"I'll tell you who does. Bill knows women. He's every kind of a bastard, that man, but you can't get away from it he does know women. Willie Strayte knows women."

"Knew women."

She glared at me out of her large, slightly protuberant blue eyes. "A man who knew women would never pick me up on a thing like that. Look at the way you treat that little girl of yours, what's her name, Rose. That girl was mad about you, Dave Nelson, probably still is."

We were sitting by ourselves at one end of the room, but Sonia's voice was loud enough to reach the men sitting up at the bar. "Pipe down, Sonia", I said and added as an afterthought, "You mean I ought to treat 'em rough, like Thorby Larsen."

She waved her brawny arm. "Not a question of treating them rough. Shall I tell you something about yourself, Dave? Behind that bright boy business executive air you're just a cold fish at heart."

"I thought you told other people I wasn't like that."

"So I do, but it's true all the same. You're a nice boy, Dave, and you've got the kind of looks I go for, but at bottom you're a cold fish."

I was pretty bored with all this. Obviously Sonia had been drinking, though you couldn't say she was drunk. I took a deep breath and jumped in with both feet. "Did you get married while Bill was in South Africa?"

To my astonishment a flush suffused Sonia's face. "Who said anything about Bill being in South Africa?"

"Why, I don't know. Bill, I expect."

"I expect", she mimicked. Her enormous cupid's bow mouth was pulled down at the corners. "And I expect somebody's trying to stick his nose in where it doesn't belong. Take care it doesn't get hurt." She doubled up her meaty fist by way of illustration.

"Sorry if I've said something I shouldn't, Sonia. Just tank up and forget it." I ordered two more doubles and said, with a fine touch of understatement, "I've been a little worried lately."

"About this Willie Strayte business, I know. Bill told me. He understood women but he was still a rat." She spoke almost absently. "We don't talk about South Africa, Bill and I. Do you know why?"

I shook my head, unwilling to check the flow of reminiscence even by a word.

"South Africa means Malan, and Malan's a bastard. You just mention Malan to Bill and watch him spit. Underneath that tough front, Bill's democratic as hell. So mention anywhere else and it's all right – Wales, Newfoundland, Nova – Nova –

"Zembla."

"Yes, or Georgia even, Bolivia, Tibet, Peru, that's all right. But South Africa, no."

"Bill's certainly been around."

She agreed with that. "Is it my turn to buy a drink?" I saw with surprise that her glass was empty.

Rather reluctantly I ordered another drink. There might be nothing in all this, but now that we were talking about South Africa I didn't want to let it go. We sipped our whisky in solemn silence for a little, then I tried again. "Bill's a kind of honorary citizen of pretty well every country in the world, isn't that so?"

"*Every* country in the world. Except South Africa. We spit on South Africa, both of us."

"Me too. I'm a democrat too." I raised my glass, Sonia raised hers, we clinked glasses.

"If there's one thing I love it's a democrat. That husband of mine now, he's a bastard but he's a democratic bastard. That's why I've stuck to him. Through thick and thin, Dave."

"Through thick and thin."

"Thick and thin. Fair weather and foul. Better or worse. And a lot of it's been worse. When's the better coming, I've asked him that a good many times in the last twenty years."

"Twenty years you've been together, is that so?"

"Twenty years", she said dreamily. I couldn't tell whether she was drunk or kidding me or telling the truth. "And every one of them happier than the last. I love that rat. Where do you suppose he is now, Dave? Important appointment, do you suppose that means another woman? I wouldn't mind, I don't care, I'd wait for him till hell freezes over. But wouldn't you say I'd be enough woman for him, wouldn't you, Dave?"

"I certainly would." She would have been enough woman for any five men I knew.

"But I don't care. Let him play around with this girl Beverley, he'll always come back to me."

"Beverley? Did you say Beverley?"

"He told me to keep it under my hat, but I never wear a hat so how can I? Beverley he said, and isn't that a girl's name, isn't there a film star with that name now?"

"Jake Beverley."

"That was the name he mentioned. Was it real, do you know a Jake Beverley, Dave?"

There seemed no reason why I shouldn't tell her, though if I hadn't had the whisky I might have kept my mouth shut. "I met someone called Jake Beverley last night. He's round as a tub and greasy with money. He was talking about starting up a new company to compete with Gross and Venturesome. I told him he was crazy, the market wouldn't stand it. I don't think I was very popular. He probably wants to talk to Bill about the same thing."

"Is that so? Is that really so?" Her eyes filled with tears and she dabbed at them with a handkerchief. "You're not kidding me?"

"I wouldn't kid you, Sonia, not about a thing like that."

"You're a lovely man, Dave. I've always said you were a lovely man. Shall I tell you a great secret, a very very great secret that you mustn't tell to a soul. About South Africa."

I hardly dared to take breath. "That's up to you."

Her eyes didn't quite focus now as she looked at me. "I expect you thought I got the needle a bit when you were talking about South Africa, isn't that so? That Sonia, you thought, she's a fairly average kind of bitch biting my head off just for mentioning South Africa. Don't deny it, I could see it in your eyes, you were hurt. Shall I tell you something about yourself Dave? You're too sensitive. You're a poet at heart." She lapsed into a brooding state, looking gloomily at her glass. "What was I saying?"

"South Africa."

"South Africa, yes. All that stuff I told you about Malan and Bill being a democrat, you didn't believe that, did you?"

"Not altogether."

"And about Bill in Bolivia and Wales, and Nova you know, and Tibet, that isn't all true, not by any means it isn't. He's been around, yes, but confidentially that bastard's never been in Tibet. South Africa, though – *yes*." There was a glaze over her eyes now, a thick glaze. "Bill certainly has been in South Africa. I shouldn't be telling you this and I wouldn't be if he hadn't stood me up. And on our wedding anniversary too, golden wedding, did I tell you that?"

"You were talking about South Africa." The whisky in my glass was a beautiful golden brown.

"South Africa. You know the thing about Bill and South Africa?" I went on looking at the whisky in my glass, holding the glass up to the light to see the colour more clearly. Somehow a little splashed over the edge on to my hand. "Bill went to prison in South Africa."

The glass bumped down on the table between us. I took my hand, wet, away from it. My hand was trembling slightly. Here it is, I said to myself, here it is.

Now Sonia spoke stridently. "Don't look at me in that tone of voice, Dave Nelson, as if I suddenly turned out to be something the cat dragged in. Bill's twice the man you'll ever be I can tell you, in prison or out of it."

"I know that." To make it sound more earnest I repeated it. "I know that, Sonia."

"I'm not sure I'll tell you any more about it. What kind of a bastard are you, anyway, sticking your nose in the air because a man's been in jug. Let me tell you, you're not sitting so pretty, Mr Nelson. Bill may have made a little mistake over cash, but he was never in anything like the spot you're in at this moment. I would *not* like to be in your shoes, David Nelson, not even the club-footed one."

"A mistake over cash. Did you say that, a mistake over cash?"

"That was the way Bill looked at it, and I did too, but you know what they did, those Cape Town bastards. They called it *em-bezz-le-ment.*" She pronounced the word carefully and correctly. "He was running a touring company. They put him away for twelve months. I waited for him, I'll always be proud that I waited for him. It was years ago now but he's been the best man any woman could want since he came out."

"Embezzlement." I felt laughter rising in my throat.

"What did you think he'd got mixed up with? Murder?"

Now the laughter rocketed out of my throat, coming up in great choking gulps like hiccoughs. I stood up and knocked my glass to the floor with my sleeve. The bar was beginning to fill up, people were looking at us. *Pull yourself together, Dave Nelson,* I said silently. *Don't want to make a public exhibition.* Sonia lay sprawled in her chair like a great bursting cushion, looking up at me with bewilderment. “A fine bastard you are, Dave Nelson. You’ve spilt whisky on my dress.”

“Embezzlement. Twelve months. Excuse me.” The laughter exploded again inside me as I made my way uncertainly across the room to the door. In the hall outside I saw Bill Rogers rolling towards me with his bow-legged walk, an uneasy grin on his face.

“How goes it, Dave old man?”

“Never better.” I burst again into a series of short explosive barks.

“Let me in on the joke.” I shook my head, helpless with laughter. “Is the little woman inside? Hell of a thing, I got held up and it’s kind of our anniversary tonight.”

“She certainly is inside, my old Cape Town cowboy.”

“What’s that you said?”

“She’s all tanked up and waiting for you, and she’s been letting off steam. Do you know how long she’s been waiting, Bill? Twelve months.”

I saw Bill’s red face, I saw his hairy fist come up. Then I felt a blow on the side of the face and had the sensation, rather pleasant, of moving through air.

Chapter Thirty-Five

"Here we are, old chap", said the taximan. "Delivered right to the door as per instructions. How are you feeling?"

I blinked outside the taxi, saw the thin lances of rain falling and recognised our block of flats. "Whose instructions?"

He was a young and slightly cultured taximan with rimless glasses. He looked as if he would have done well as assistant to Charles Peers. "Your friends at the Rubicon Club, sir. I gathered there had been what you might call a bit of a fracas. Just horseplay, you know. They were very solicitous, asked me to see you into your flat if necessary."

"Not necessary at all. I feel fine."

"I'm sure you do, sir." He laughed encouragingly, in a professionally medical kind of way. "Out you come."

It was perfectly true that I felt all right while I sat down, but as soon as I began to walk a dull hammer began to beat in my forehead. I didn't exactly need help, but I didn't raise any objection to his following me up the stairs. I could hear voices inside the flat, but couldn't make out whose they were.

"Are you married, sir?" It was the taximan behind me.

"Yes. Why?"

"Merely as well to have a suitable answer when asked what happened to your eye. 'The floor came up and hit me' is always one that should raise a laugh if your wife has a sense of humour."

"Thanks."

"If you haven't any steak for that eye, and which of us has nowadays, I recommend ice or half a raw onion. Shall I put the key in the lock for you?"

"Thanks." He still hovered around. "What now?"

"Shall I just straighten the old tie, sir?" He did so and coughed apologetically. "The fare. Three and sixpence on the meter."

I gave him five shillings and he seemed delighted. Then I turned the key, opened the door, and went into the sitting room. The tableau that met my eyes was one that at first I refused to believe. It seemed part of a general unreality in my experiences. I blinked at it, but it did not change.

Rose sat in an armchair with her legs curled under her, smoking a cigarette. Her expression was lively, and even gay. James and Marian sat together on the sofa, James looking as if he had been listening to a wireless programme on recent trends in music, Marian knitting a shapeless mauve-coloured garment. And sitting opposite Rose in my armchair, twinkling with oily good nature, was Jake Beverley.

The general air of animation and good humour about the scene changed abruptly at my appearance. Rose's expression became immediately anxious and distressed, as if I looked even worse than she had expected. James' mouth fell slightly open – in his case it was rather as though his Third Programme talk had given way to bebop. Marian lowered her head and stabbed savagely with the knitting needles. Only Beverley gave me an unperturbed fat beam of welcome.

"Dave, what's happened?" Rose moved over to my side with a show of solicitude that impressed me as stagey.

"The floor came up and hit me."

Marian sniffed. James seemed to consider the statement, and closed his mouth with a disapproving snap. Rose said, "Don't be a fool. You've been in a fight."

Evidently she had no sense of humour. "I was in a fight with Thorby Larsen. He won."

"Oh, Dave, just look at yourself." She led me to a glass. Bill Rogers had obviously been wearing a ring, for there was a cut over my eyebrow. My eye was not yet discoloured, but it would be purplish in the morning. My knuckles, to my surprise, were slightly lacerated and my suit was quite remarkably dirty. Clearly I had made some resistance to Bill Rogers' attack. Or there had been, as the taximan well put it, a little horseplay.

"A little horseplay", I said. "If no steak is available half a raw onion or a slab of ice is recommended by the best authorities." I said to Beverley, "To what do I owe this pleasure? You seem to have come in on a family party."

"Mr Beverley has been telling us of his experiences in the City", Marian said in her prim voice. "Most interesting."

"Absorbingly so", James whinnied. "I had no idea the adventures of high finance were so romantic."

"There's romance everywhere if you look for it", I said. "Suppose you two go and look for a little romance in Croydon right away."

"Dave", cried Rose.

"Take no notice", Marian said calmly. "He's been drinking."

Beverley hoisted himself out of my chair and spoke a little breathlessly. "Don't be hard on Dave, ladies. What if he has taken a drop? I only wish I could take it myself without feeling like a sick cat. The flesh is willing but my ulcers say no. I well remember when I fixed the merger of my universal Household Goods with Barney Ballato's Multiple Displays Limited – that was worth a million and a half to me, that merger – Barney said to me, 'Change a lifelong custom, Jake, and take a drink.' I said to him – mind you, he'd signed on the dotted line by then – 'Barney boy, do you know why I'm buying you up instead of you buying me, when you can outsmart me any day of the week? It's this little ulcer I've got just here.' " He tapped his great stomach. " 'The ulcer stops me drinking and tells me when I'm acting foolish. I tell you honest, Barney, I reckon that ulcer's worth five million pound to me'. That's what I said to Barney Ballato – and yet suppose you offered me my health and strength wouldn't I take it? What's money after all? It can't buy health, it can't buy happiness, and you can't take it with you."

I stood looking out of the window. Beverley's car was standing in the rain. "A Rolls", I murmured.

"What's that?"

"It can buy you a Rolls."

There was a hostile silence behind my back. Then Rose's voice, clear and cold, said, "You wanted to talk to Dave alone, Mr Beverley, didn't you? We'll wait in the bedroom."

I didn't turn round. "Don't strain your good nature, Rose. If you feel you have to go to Croydon with them, don't let me stop you."

I heard a door closing. Then Beverley's voice, rich and oily. "Cigarette, Davy boy? You don't smoke cigars, am I right?"

I took a cigarette from a black enamel case studded with what looked like diamonds. The lighter was black with diamonds to match.

"I got a hundred other things to remember, and yet I remembered that. Not bad, eh?"

"Remarkable." My eye ached but my head, astonishingly, felt perfectly clear. He waited for me to ask what he'd come to see me about. I didn't oblige him.

"You know what Barney Ballato said to me at the end of that conversation I was telling you about? 'Jake', he said, 'The man who could outsmart you deserves the VC.' " Beverley chuckled fatly, then became grave. "Have you thought over our talk last night?"

"Should I have done? What is there to think about?" He nodded admiringly. "I didn't make a firm offer, that's what you mean, isn't it? You certainly play 'em close to the chest, Davy boy, but mind I admire you for it."

"I don't know what you're talking about."

"You don't, eh? Here it is, then, as straight as Jake Beverley can make it. Five hundred pounds by cheque, fivers, or in five hundred oncers if that's the way you want it, for your story."

"My story?"

"The story of you and Gross Enterprises, the story of just how tough it is up at the top of the tree in that kind of business, the way a Thorby Larsen book gets written, the way the machine works. And the story of how Willie Strayte dished you for the editorship of that magazine, the story of Willie's murder and what came after it. That's a straight offer, and if you're half the man I think you are, Davy boy, you'll shake hands on it."

I passed my hand over my forehead, and winced as it touched my eye. "Let me get this clear. You're seriously offering me five hundred pounds for my story." Beverley nodded. His eyes, twinkling in their mask of flesh, watched me intently. "It doesn't make sense. You'd want it for this new firm you're thinking about, is that right?"

"I want the rights in it. If I can't use the story one way, I can use it another."

"You know what my position is? I'm a suspect in a murder case, I might be arrested tomorrow."

"You can still write the story. Couldn't you use five hundred pounds for your defence? Mind, Davy boy, that's looking on the black side. If the police have got half the sense I think they have they'll know a smart boy like you had nothing to do with it."

I thought it out aloud. "If you did follow up this crazy idea you've got of starting a new company in competition with Gross and Venturesome you couldn't get it going for six months. Any story of mine would be stale by then. So you must think you can use it somehow to stick a knife into Gross Enterprises where it hurts. But how would you do it? And what good would it do you to damage Gross, when you haven't got an organization ready to take over from them?" Beverley simply sat and watched me. "I'd write this story myself – that's understood?"

"Where could I get a better man?"

"What about my wife? She comes into it in a way."

"She's a real peach." Beverley's face glowed for a moment in appreciation of her peachiness. "Your personal life, that's between you and her and the gatepost. I wouldn't want to pry into that. It's the other side of it I want."

"Much appreciated." I could hear no sound from the bedroom. I wondered whose ear was at the keyhole. "Frankly I think you're crazy. But I'll take your offer, I'll take that five hundred pounds. And if you ever start the new company I'll take the job too, fifty per cent over my present salary as you said."

"I knew you were smart, Davy boy. Shake hands on it." We shook hands.

"What happens now? Do you bring an agreement out of your pocket so that I can sign it in triplicate."

He laughed heartily. "Not in triplicate, but just as a matter of form." He took from his pocket a manila envelope and extracted one sheet of paper. It simply assigned rights in my life story, including an account of my career at Gross Enterprises and my relations with Willie Strayte, to Jacob Beverley. I signed it, he signed it, and then he put it back in the manila envelope and the envelope into his pocket.

"How about the five hundred oncers?"

He laughed happily. "You're right after it, you don't miss a trick. It's a pleasure to do business with you. I'll be in touch with you tomorrow and you'll get your money, don't worry about that."

The whole thing was ludicrous. I still had it in my mind that he was an escaped lunatic, Rolls and all. "How did you get on with Bill Rogers? Did you offer him five hundred for his life story, too?"

"Right after it, like I said." In Beverley's voice there was no surprise, nothing but admiration. "Yes. I saw Bill tonight and he's coming in if we can fix things up. He's a good boy, Bill, and dead smart with it, so Charlie Peers tells me. Takes a high view of you, Davy. I can tell you that."

"He gave me a present tonight to show his brotherly love." I pointed to my eye. "Next time you see him remember to ask how he liked life in South Africa."

"Ah, you're too deep for me. Never had the benefits of schooling, you know. Nothing can make up for that." He got up out of my armchair and said solemnly, "Making 'em stop at school till they're fifteen is the greatest thing that's happened in this country in the last few years. I left when I was twelve. If I'd only had those three years extra schooling, Davy, I might have done something in life." He waited for me to say he had done something and then said with some disappointment, "I ought to be getting along, but first I must pay my respects to your lady."

I threw open the door of the bedroom. Rose was sitting at the dressing table looking at herself critically in the glass. Marian was knitting, and James crouched by a small cupboard that contained a dozen Gross publications.

"Mr Beverley wants to say goodbye."

Beverley came into the room, shook hands with Marian and James, seized Rose's hand, bent down with difficulty, and kissed it. Then he waddled away to his Rolls.

Chapter Thirty-Six

When he had gone we stayed fixed in our positions – another tableau, this time a family scene out of the *New Yorker.* Rose sat staring into the rimless triple mirror above her fumed oak kneehole dressing table. Her reflection looked thoughtful, upper teeth reflectively nipping lower lip. The mauve knitting over which Marian brooded contrasted hideously with the pink chair in which she sat. James had his goat-head in a paper-backed book. I caught sight of myself in Rose's mirror, a vague-eyed dusty prodigal returned to this homey scene.

James gave a sudden, surprising bleat. "Extraordinary, quite extraordinary. I really had no idea – " He held up the book he had been snuffling at and I saw that it was *Hit to Death* by Thorby Larsen. "Is this – ah – Thorby Larsen a real writer?"

"He's real enough, but there are about half a dozen parts of him. That particular Thorby Larsen was mostly written by someone named Birkett. Another man named George Pacey and I added some trimmings."

"Quite remarkable", James bleated. "There's a directness about the style, a tension and force – "

"Force all right. In that book the hero Punch Sheldon kills three of the crooks with his bare hands."

"Yes, yes, I understand that there is a necessary superstructure of melodrama, but the style itself has a primitive violence and power which – " James lapsed into muttering. "A genuine popular art", he said eventually. "Myth of the collective unconscious. May I borrow this? I feel it would repay study."

"I don't know what you're talking about, but borrow it by all means. You'll find some more there. Come in and see Birkett some time, I'm sure he'd appreciate anything you can tell him about the collective unconscious."

James put some of the books into his pockets and got up. "A most interesting man, Mr Beverley."

"Yes, a vital type. The attendant was waiting in the car to take him back to Colney Hatch."

James looked puzzled. Marian, as she put away her knitting into a great loose bag, seemed almost to be afraid. "Rose, darling, are you sure – "

Rose's voice was muffled. "I'm all right."

"You really want us to go?"

"Yes."

"You can come back with us if you feel – "

I said politely. "Your kind offer has been refused. Don't let me detain you."

"Rose, I don't feel that we should leave you like this. Whatever you may think, I'm not sure that David is to be relied upon."

"Oh, go on, Marian. Don't fuss." Rose got up and opened the door into the living-room.

Maintaining my politeness. I saw them off the premises and even walked downstairs with them. At the entrance to the flats I said, "Goodbye. Have a nice journey home."

Marian turned round and faced me. "I don't like you, David Nelson, and you know it. But let me tell you something. You think Rose has behaved badly to you, you've got a wonderful sense of injured innocence, but let me tell you it's nothing to the way you've behaved to her. And you're quite convinced of your own cleverness, aren't you? There's nobody smarter than David Nelson."

"I'm just a genuine popular artist", I said modestly. "With a clubfoot. Ask James here."

"Oh, what's the use, how can anybody talk to you? Come along, James." I watched them walking down the street together, goat-faced James with copies of Thorby Larsen's books in his hairy old tweed overcoat, dumpy thick-legged Marian with the mauve knitting in her bag. Then I went upstairs again. On the way up I thought about what Marian had said, and wondered what she was trying to say. Was it true about Rose, had I behaved badly, had I got a sense of injured innocence? My eye ached, and I gave up the problem. What was the use of thinking about it, anyway?

Entering the flat again I was met by a mouse-like scratching. It took me a moment or two to identify the sound. In the bedroom Rose still sat before the triple mirror, but she was now filing her nails. The blank look on her face made me a little uncomfortable.

"Time for that eye poultice. Is there some steak and onion in the house?" She did not reply. "You notice I ask no questions about just where you went this afternoon, having made the deduction all on my own that you were with Maid Marian. Right?"

"Yes."

"You're not very communicative. Don't you want to know what Dumb Crambo said to me? Or how I got on with Jumping Jake, the Terror of the City? He offered me five hundred pounds for my life story." Still she said nothing. "For God's sake stop filing your damned nails."

Rose's eyes stared intently at me in the mirror – or was she in fact simply looking into vacancy? I could not be sure. The words she spoke were carefully enunciated. "I'm going to have a baby, Dave."

I sat down on the bed and gaped at her back which was directed towards me with what seemed purposeful hostility. I could not take in the meaning of the words.

She repeated them, in that careful way. "I'm going to have a baby."

I had to make a conscious effort, so that the Dave Nelson I'd built up over the years shouldn't collapse. "Tremendous news. But why tell me, after all? Isn't it a charge on Willie Strayte's estate?"

I suppose I must have wanted to needle her into losing her temper, but I didn't succeed. In the same voice she asked, "Is that all you want to say, Dave?"

When I put my hand to my forehead it touched my eye, and I winced. There were all sorts of things I wanted to say, but I didn't know how to say them and I wasn't even sure what they were. "Look, Rose, I've got a lot of things on my mind. I'm the chap who found Christy Freeman's body today. Remember you lent a helping hand? The police seem to think there's something suspicious about that, don't like people coming across bodies in that sort of way. Didn't like my cigarette lighter being under the divan either – remember the one you gave me? He's funny that way, Inspector Crambo, seems to think I planted it there myself and then let him know about it. There are a lot of other funny people about too. Bill Rogers, you know Bill, now he's done time in South Africa. And that fat ape who was in here dazzling your beloved sister with tales of the City, God knows what *his* game is or where I'm mixed up in it." She listened without moving, staring straight ahead of her in the glass. "What do you expect me to say, Rose? How happy I shall be to father Willie's bastard?"

Now at last she turned round on the seat. Her face was grave and even a little sad, but composed. "And if I swear to you that I know this is your child and not Willie Strayte's?"

"Do you swear that?" I asked curiously.

She spoke still without a flicker of emotion, but her hand gripped tightly the side of the stool on which she sat. "I always took precautions with Willie. Do you think I'd have wanted his child, or that he'd have wanted it either? But with you at the end – well, I didn't."

"You wanted to keep a hold on me one way or another, eh?"

"I knew it would be a good thing. The only thing that could help us perhaps."

I paused, waiting for the next words to come out. When they came they seemed to have no relation to what I was thinking. "How many men do you think would believe this tale? You must take me for a prize fool."

"You never take yourself for any kind of a fool, do you?"

"I don't know what you mean."

"It doesn't matter. You know it's true, don't you, you know I'm telling the truth."

I said angrily, too angrily, "I don't know anything of the sort. I don't see how I can."

"Can you look at me and say you don't believe me? But it doesn't matter, let it go." She got up, came over to the bed, and with a sleepwalker's unconscious efficiency began to pack clothes neatly into a case. "Did you ever love me, Dave? I don't think you ever did."

Dave Nelson, I cried despairingly and silently, *Dave Nelson where are you now, what are you going to say?* "I love you now", I said.

"You always wanted proof of my love, I had to take yours for granted. Isn't that true?"

"I don't know what you're talking about. Where are you going?"

"Down to Marian. She was quite right, she always said it would end this way. She went with me to the doctor's this afternoon to make certain. She wanted me to go back with her at once and not stay to see you, but I said no."

"You said no."

"I said if you loved me, if you'd ever loved me, you'd know I was telling you the truth."

She went on packing. Love, I said to myself as I watched her, what's love, can two human beings ever love one another? Desire yes, and companionship, but what is love? And as I watched her I felt something – how can I put it – it was as though something broke inside me. I didn't know whether I believed her or not, any more than I had done when she first spoke, but I felt a rush of warmth and a slackening of tension that came out in words. "Rose, don't go. I believe you, I do truly believe you. Let's have our pink sugar princess, Evangeline her name's got to be." She did not answer. "Rose, listen to what I'm saying."

"I'm listening."

"I'm saying let's do it your way Rose, let's do what you want. Have the baby and to hell with it."

She stayed composed, apparently indifferent. I'd never seen her like it. "To hell with what? I'm having the baby, if that's what you mean. You can get a divorce, I shan't fight it."

"Oh Rose, Rose." I stood up and took her in my arms. She did not resist, she stayed in my arms like a dummy. When I released her she went on packing. I took out the clothes and threw them on the floor. She calmly picked them up again.

"It's too late now. You don't love me or you wouldn't talk about doing it my way. It should be our way, not mine. You don't believe me."

"I do believe you, I do, I do." I felt tears rolling down my cheeks. Another part of me – and which part was Dave Nelson? – said this was all ridiculous, a scene from the hammiest kind of melodrama. "Darling Rose, I don't want us to break up. I want to have our little baby, little Evangeline."

"It might not be Evangeline." It seemed the first crack in her calm.

"Adam then, Adam the original sinner. Didn't I say we might have a little baby, that's before I knew about this? Didn't I say I wanted it? Don't break up now, let's try together. You've been right all the time, this is just what we needed. How far gone is it?"

"Just far enough to be sure. I don't know, Dave, I just don't know."

I found myself almost incoherent with excitement. "It's what we've always wanted really, Rose, both of us. We were fools not to before, I was a fool I mean. This deserves a celebration, let's just go out and celebrate, have a real blind, we haven't done that for ages." I stopped suddenly. "Is that all right for you? I mean in your condition – "

She burst out laughing. "You're too funny, Dave", she said between bursts of laughter. "Too sweet, you really are. My condition's fine. Let's go out then, but not on a blind. Let's go to the Follies."

"The Follies", I said rapturously. "Let's go to the Follies."

"I'll be ready in five minutes. And Dave, darling, you'd better put on another suit and bathe that eye. Or shall I bathe it for you?"

"I can do it. You go and make yourself look glamorous, little mother."

I was going out to the bathroom. Rose stopped me at the door. "You're sure this is the way you want it? Sure you believe in me?"

I laughed, with no sense of strain. "Hell, Rosie, I'm no first prize. If you can believe in me, can't I believe in you?"

Outside in the bathroom I washed my knuckles and cleaned up the cut over my eye so that it didn't look too bad. Dave Nelson, I said to myself in the glass, who are you fooling? What do you believe and what don't you believe and what do you really want? I hadn't got any answers to those questions, I'd never had any answers to them, they weren't questions that bothered me in a general way. And they didn't much bother me now, they were just specks in the wild, unreasoning happiness I felt.

Chapter Thirty-Seven

The Follies Club has its home in a street just off the Charing Cross Road. You go down some awkward steps and through a door which leads to an anteroom made up to look like a Victorian parlour, with aspidistras and antimacassars, a set of mahogany chairs with legs carved into the shape of animals, dark flowered wallpaper, a huge horsehair sofa covered with mahogany Cupids, and one of those love seats nobody can sit on.

Beyond this anteroom is the main clubroom with a small stage at one end of it. In the rest of the room is more Victorian furniture, chairs and tables and sofas, all of them covered with scrollwork and carved with Cupids, antlers flowers and figures of Prince Albert and Queen Victoria. There is a bar at one end called "The Gin Palace", which is all over prismatic glass, and is lighted by gas jets.

It was all supposed to be like a Victorian supper club. Men and women came out on to the stage and sang Victorian songs and if you wanted to you joined in. And the people who went there did want to join in, that was the kind of people they were, and the way they convinced themselves that they were having a hell of a time and being tremendously Bohemian. Rose was tickled pink by it, but I wasn't. I always used to say that I was several kinds of a phoney, but not quite as phoney as that. So it was a kind of peace offering on my part, or something like that, to go to the Follies.

Bohemian or not, Rose had really got herself up to go places in an off-the-shoulder black evening dress that seemed to be semi-transparent down to the waist. I should have put on my dinner jacket to keep her company, but couldn't quite bring myself to it. I compromised on a double-breasted very plain dark suit with white shirt and pearl grey tie, that I always thought made me look a pretty neat trick.

We checked our coats and went in. As we were going in a man brushed past us on his way out, a man with straw-coloured hair who looked a bit out of place at the Follies, though for the matter of that you got all sorts there. The appearance of this man jangled away at something inside my head. What it was I just didn't know, but it had something to do with the death of Christy Freeman. We went inside and sat down at a table carved in pretty well every conceivable place, and covered with bits of mother-of-pearl in the spots they'd accidentally left uncarved. The chairs we sat in had fairly comfortable padded seats but their backs were made to represent antlers and reminded you quite often that antlers had points. People who went to the Follies thought it was fun to be jabbed in the back by wooden antlers.

The tables for two were all occupied, so we sat at one for four. Two people were there already, a queeny young man wearing drainpipe trousers, and a fat ruddy melancholy middle-aged figure in a tweed suit. When the melancholy man spoke to the young queen I noticed his Northern accent. I put them down as advertising agent and client. I got two drinks from the imitation gin palace and settled down for a bad couple of hours. When I got back to the table Rose had already got into conversation with the others. That's the kind of place the Follies Club is, chummy.

"I'm Potter", the middle aged-man said. "Peter Potter's Powders, keep your dog's coat sleek as silk. Reckon you've heard of 'em."

"Oh yes", Rose said vaguely. "My husband, David Nelson."

"Glad to know you. Mr Potter's handshake was hearty. "This here's the young man does our advertising, Norman Wilson. Good thing you said you'd heard of our powders, Mrs Nelson. Money we spend on advertising everyone should have heard of 'em, that's what I say. Norman here's showing me a bit of life now. I like to see a bit of something different when I come up to London."

Norman smiled at us in a superior way. Right first time, Dave Nelson, I said to myself. Manufacturer and advertising agent it is. One up to you.

A savage-looking figure in ragged clothes, dirty-faced, with a battered hat on his head, came on to the stage and looked at us with loathing, a look which was greeted with a roar of delighted laughter. The man took an old pipe out of his mouth, knocked it against his heel, and began to chant in a rusty voice:

My name it is Sam Hall, I'm a thief!
My name it is Sam Hall, I'm a thief!
  My name it is Sam Hall,
  And I've robbed both great and small
  And my greeting is to all,
Damn your eyes!

The song was popular here. I had often heard it before. Almost everyone sang it. Rose sang it with her eyes closed, and a look of rapture on her face. Potter broke off from bellowing the words to say, "It's right down immoral, this place. We've got nothing like it up north, I'll give you that." An old dowager type, crusty with jewels, chanted solemnly, "My name it is Sam Hall, I'm a thief." Foxy-looking young men with demure peachy girls sang it, porty old Colonels sang it, bewildered but delighted foreigners sang it. Norman Wilson sang it in a light high voice. I sang it myself. The first verse was repeated, and then a horsy man wearing a red and blue peaked jockey's cap cried: "Come on, Joe. Let's have it. *They've shut me up in quod.*"

The laughter rose higher as the man on the stage spat deliberately within a foot of the dowager. The old lady's face was purple with pleasure. The man sang the next verse:

They've shut me up in quod, up in quod,
They've shut me up in quod, up in quod,
  They've shut me up in quod
  For killing of a sod
  They have, so help me God,
Damn their eyes!

Rose opened her eyes and smiled at me. I smiled back at her. Potter said: "Young people enjoying themselves, I like to see it."

The place was full of cigarette smoke. I peered through it and said, "I'll be damned". A stout squat figure had just come in and was waddling purposefully among the tables. It was Beverley. I pressed Rose's foot under the table. She looked at me enquiringly. "Over there", I said. She pressed my foot in return, and her smile widened.

"Friendly here", said Potter. "I like to be friendly. Let's have a drink together. Norman boy, get us a bottle of bubbly. I'm parched." Norman Wilson waved a thin white hand to a hard-pressed waiter. "You keep a dog?" Potter asked Rose.

"No."

"You're wrong there. Every young couple should have a dog."

The man on the stage chanted in a gloomy monotone:

The parson he will come, he will come,
The parson he will come, he will come,
  The Parson he will come,
  And he'll look so bloody glum,
  And he'll talk of Kingdom Come –
Damn his eyes!

Champagne fizzed in four glasses. "Here's to your powders, Mr Potter", said Rose.

"Here's to the dashing dogs who take them", I added. I was peering through the smoke, trying to see Beverley.

Potter laughed uproariously. "Ah, this is the life, you know how to live down here all right. *The Parson he will come, And he'll look so bloody glum.* Did you ever know a parson didn't look glum, now?"

Norman Wilson said in a ladylike voice, "Really, of course, we should be eating oysters and welsh rarebits and drinking stout and all that sort of thing, if we *really* wanted to reproduce the Victorian supper club atmosphere. Nobody in a place like this ever drank *champagne.*"

I stood up and said to Rose, "Back in a minute." Then I walked across the floor, in the general direction taken by Beverley. As I moved along in a blue haze, fragments of conversation drifted up at me from the tables I passed:

"...it's a gamble, so what, isn't life a gamble too?"

"...the British have always been sentimental about niggers"

"...we're not all slaves to the Yankee dollar yet, I said, so keep your paws to yourself"

"...the parson he will come, he will come"

"...the interesting thing was that you could see literally right through her"

"...The Yanks on one side, the Russians on the other, and we're just Mister in Between"

"...Miss, you mean"

"...given us freedom to buy what we like, is that wrong?"

"...and he'll look so bloody glum"

"...my trouble's always been psychological, I said, I just don't seem to have any aggressive instincts"

Walking along head in air, eye throbbing, I heard all this and much more. Then a word came out of this fog of conversation that matched the fog of smoke. "Dave."

I stopped and looked down. At a table just by the stage were three people I should never have expected to see together. Jake Beverley was one of them. He had called my name, and now he beamed at me fatly. He looked happy. With him at the table, and looking as cheerful as lobsters who've just been dropped into the pot, were Jack Dimmock and Sir Henry.

"Sit down, Davy boy", said Jake Beverley. He patted a chair. "Honoured to have you in my little establishment. Yes, I own this place, don't look so surprised, didn't I tell you I was everywhere the cash register is ringing? Not that there's any money in this, you understand, just a bit of fun. Sit down, Davy boy, you're welcome. What will you have to drink?"

In front of Beverley there was a glass of milk, in front of Sir Henry a glass of water, in front of Jack Dimmock the remains of a glass of sherry. It didn't look much like fun. I said I would have a gin and french. The battered singer moved towards us, and Beverley waved an arm. "Get away a bit, Joe, we want to hear ourselves think." The man turned and moved away, halted, and sang in a voice that sounded like a rusty saw cutting wood:

The sheriff he'll come too, he'll come too,
The sheriff he'll come too, he'll come too,
  The sheriff he'll come too,
  With all his ghastly crew,
  Their bloody work to do,
Damn their eyes!

There was no singing at our table. Jack Dimmock bent his thick brows on me. "So you decided to help scuttle the ship, eh, Dave?"

"I don't know what you mean."

"Like hell you don't. Is Beverley here right when he says you've signed that bit of paper he showed us, promising to give the low-down on our outfit and the way it works, and all this dirty business about Willie Strayte?"

"Yes. But – "

"What kind of effect do you think that's going to have on sales, when it appears in a magazine?"

"I don't know what you mean", I said again. I repeated the argument I'd used earlier to Beverley himself. "Beverley's starting from scratch. He can't get anything running for another six months. By that time my story will have about as much news value as queen Victoria's Diamond Jubilee. Even if he could use it now in some other way, what good would that do him when he's got no organization ready to take over from you?"

"Have you ever heard that we've got a rival? The name is Venturesome."

"But Venturesome's run by Arthur Lake. He started it on a shoestring." My voice faded away.

Beverley chuckled, sipped his milk. "Not since four months ago, Davy boy. I own Venturesome."

Sir Henry sighed and looked down hopelessly at his glass of water. Jack Dimmock laid the whole thing out for me in short, biting phrases. It seemed that he controlled himself only by an effort.

"He owns Venturesome. So he *has* got an organization. He's all set to take over if we fold up. More than that. He's shown us the mock-up of a magazine they'll produce to fight our *Crime Magazine*. Your autobiography will go in the first issue. I hope you're getting well paid for it, Dave."

"My boys always get well paid", said Beverley.

"They should do. Thirty pieces of silver or something. You've got one black eye, Dave. If I hadn't lost the heart for it I'd try and make it two."

Now I had the feeling somebody had spoken of to me in the last day or two, the feeling of being trapped in a constantly contracting space where there was practically no room at all to move, no escape from what none of us find easy to contemplate – ourselves. I said feebly: "Hell, how was I to know?"

Gross spoke in his voice, thin and reedy as a worn gramophone record. "There is such a thing as loyalty, young man."

"I don't see where loyalty comes into it. Beverley fooled me, I admit it. I thought he was crazy. But he's fooled you too, just as much. He's got half your staff by promising to pay fancy prices. You were neck deep in trouble before I signed this paper, now you're up to the eyes, that's all the difference. And why shouldn't I sign it? What do I owe Gross Enterprises but hard work for my monthly cheque? You want my resignation you can have it, but let's not have this stuff about loyalty." I drained the gin and french and reflected that I had nothing to lose.

Then as up the drop I go, up I go,
Then as up the drop I go, up I go,
    Then as up the drop I go,
    The swine down there below
    Will say 'We told you so',
Damn their eyes!

As up the drop I go, up I go. The words went round and round in my head and were joined there with something else. Hard to say exactly what I felt. The usual sensation you have when you've been absolutely fooled as I had been, but something else too, a feeling that everything I was doing and saying and listening – had a meaning I couldn't fathom.

"Just look at Professor Clode over there", Beverley said amiably. "Very brilliant man they tell me, professor of economics or sociology or some such stuff. Would you believe it, he comes here every night, knows 'Sam Hall' better than old Joe who sings it, often leads the choruses."

The professor, a small plump man with a pointed beard, was singing 'As up the drop I go, up I go' and making the appropriate gestures of adjusting the rope round his neck and rolling his eyes to indicate the agonies of hanging. Two pretty girls at his table were rocking with laughter.

"Can't see any humour myself in a man kicking the bucket", Beverley said. "But there you are, I never had any education."

I got up. "I must go. My wife will be wondering – "

"Your wife's a peach. But women are like good wine, they improve with keeping. Sit down." Beverley was beaming up at me, but there was something about his voice that made me sit down. "I don't like to hear that talk about resigning, Davy boy. I appeal to my friends here whether they like it either."

Dimmock seemed to unzip his lips to say "No." Sir Henry was arranging bread pellets in the shape of a B, with fingers that shook a little.

"Sorry to hear that. What makes you the spokesman?" I asked the question, though I knew the answer.

Beverley spread out his hands. "We're all one big happy family. All for one and one for all. Isn't that so, gentlemen?"

Dimmock unzipped his lips again in a yes. Sir Henry just looked sad.

"I'm anticipating in saying that, but negotiations have been going on now for a day or two. I don't mind telling you they're pretty well completed on terms agreeable to everybody. I'm telling you that, Davy boy, because you're one of the family too. At least, I hope you are."

I heard Professor Clode's characteristic high-pitched whinny of laughter, familiar from many a radio programme. One of the girls with him, a thin large-eyed brunette, had an arm round the Professor's plump shoulders and was bawling into his ear: "They've shut me up in quod, for killing of a sod." The professor did his hanging act, and they both screamed with laughter.

"What about that agreement we signed?"

Beverley's beam grew wider. "I wouldn't want to use a story like that to stab my friends in the back, would I?"

"No agreement, no life story, no five hundred oncers out of your wallet?"

"I didn't say that. Sometimes it can be more profitable not to use stuff than to use it. And I'll see you're not the loser. You put it on the line with Jake Beverley and he'll put it on the line with you, Davy boy, and no man can say different."

I felt drunk and deceived and unhappy, and I wanted to get back to Rose. "Let me lay it on the line then, Jake. You're the money behind Venturesome, which is a fact everybody seems to have known except me. When Willie Strayte was killed you saw a chance to use his death as a lever to get hold of Gross Enterprises. You made some of the top executives at Gross good offers, and you were able to widen the cracks that were bound to show in the organization in the confusion after Willie's death. Signing up my story was just the last straw added to the pile that broke the camel's back, no more than that. But when you've got control of the whole caboodle, what happens then?" I said to Dimmock and Sir Henry, "If you'll take my advice you ought to call his bluff. He's got no more intention of paying fifty per cent increased salary than he had of paying me the five hundred pounds he promised."

Sir Henry had now made his bread pellets into an X. Jack Dimmock stared at me. "You talk too much, Dave. You've got too many ideas."

He seemed more put out than Beverley, who chuckled. "Make allowances for the boy, he's had a hard day and he's got troubles. You get back to your little wife now, Dave, and say you're returned in good order, with my compliments. Come and see me in a couple of days' time when you're not feeling so hot under the collar. I'll be around."

"You said I should lay it on the line," I said uncertainly.

"And you did just that, and I respect you for it. Good night."

I stood up with the feeling that I ought to say something else, but there seemed nothing to say. I crossed the floor again, a little unsteadily. Professor Clode was now in a fierce clinch with the blonde girl. Some people get the best of everything.

I found Potter resting his head on Rose's bare shoulder, while Norman Wilson was talking to a man I recognised without any particular surprise as Charles Peers. Charles raised a hand in friendly greeting, and I caught a fragment of his conversation with Wilson: "A vulgarisation, of course... Richard Doyle's drawing... Thackeray... the Cider Cellars." It was enough.

There were three champagne bottles on the table, two empty and one half full. I poured myself a drink from this bottle and drank it at a gulp. It was unpleasantly sweet. The ruffianly figure on the stage was singing the last verse of "Sam Hall", stamping his feet and showing his teeth at the audience. They stamped their feet too, that was a highly popular routine. Rose and Potter dreamily sang the last verse together:

And now I'm going to hell, going to hell!
And now I'm going to hell, going to hell!
  And now I'm going to hell,
  But what a bloody sell
  If you all go there as well!
Damn your eyes!

Potter saw me and lifted his head abruptly from Rose's shoulder. One side of his face was covered with white powder. "Don't get any wrong ideas, lad. Your lady wife and I were just having a bit of conversation, nothing else to it. She's a wonderful woman, your wife."

"You've been a long time", Rose said.

"Just long enough to lose five hundred pounds. Let's go home."

"Powder my nose", she said and walked over to a door that said in Gothic lettering, *Ladies, Women and Gels.*

I said to Charles Peers. "Just been having a chat with our new board of directors, blotted my copybook I'm afraid."

"Are there anything but blots in your copybook, Dave?" He sounded pretty distant.

"Don't know. Here and now I'm slightly drunk. Just drunk enough to ask again about that election."

His spectacles had slipped right down his nose, he was a little drunk himself perhaps. "What's that? My only interests are art and cash, not politics."

"Not talking about politics. Our election, Willie Strayte, when I didn't get the job, remember?"

He wrinkled his nose. "Christ, you're a bore, Dave. If I said there never was any election, would that make you happy?"

"No."

"Be unhappy, then." He turned away from me and began to talk to Norman Wilson again. They seemed to be discussing Indian temples, from what I could hear of it. Rose came back looking bright and fresh.

"Good night", I said to Potter. "Thanks for the champagne."

"Here's a dog before he takes Potter's Powders. Bow-wow. And after. *Bow-wow.*" He made a thin mewling sound for the first "bow-wow" and a ferocious rattling bark for the second.

Wilson looked at him in disgust. "That's the way he always is. And this is only the beginning, my dears. We're going on to a night club now, he'll pass out there and I shall have to get him to bed. Horrid, really. Up in Rochdale or Wigan or wherever it is he's so *respectable.*"

Potter bent to kiss Rose's hand and almost fell over. "Dear lady. Remember – a doggy home is a happy home."

"I'll remember", said Rose. "Good night."

On the way home in the taxi she put her head on my shoulder. "Lovely it was. So gay. And such a funny man, that Peter Potter. Why did we have to go so soon? And where did you get to all the time?" I told her. "Oh well, I never believed in that money, did you?"

"I suppose not. What I don't like is being made to look a fool."

"No you never liked that, did you? Poor Dave. Why don't you and I and Adam get out of it all and live in a caravan?"

"Evangeline, don't forget her. And what should we live on, who'd pay for your nylons?"

"I'm a bare-legged girl at heart. I can do without nylons."

"I don't believe it. Another funny thing, did you hear what Charles Peers said about the election?" I told her that too.

"Probably a bit squiffy like the rest of us. I mean it, Dave, about that caravan. I'm not drunk now, I'm just sensible."

"You wouldn't want it any more than I should. Think of the draughts, pumping the primus in winter, the nappies spread all over the bunks."

"You don't want anything, do you, except what you've got? You love it really, isn't that right. I'm not drunk, Dave, just a little sad."

"Of course you're not drunk. You're the wife of a murder suspect with one eye that's crying out for steak. That's enough to upset any woman."

Within my arm Rose shivered. "Didn't she look terrible in that flat? Do you know, I've never seen anybody who died that way before. Violently, I mean." When we were back in the flat she said, "Kiss me. Hold me tight. Are you sure you love me?"

"Sure."

"Say it, I want you to say it."

"I love you, Rose." What was it that Charles Peers had said that day at lunch? About the circle narrowing so much that only one action appeared possible, no choice of action remained. Or was I really trying to think of something Crambo had said about a circle, what was it? And what was Rose saying?

"And you want to go on with Adam? You really believe me, honestly and truly. Because if you don't I can go back to Marian, she'll have me, you needn't be afraid I shall starve by the wayside."

I held up three fingers. "One, I love you, always have. Two, I want to go on with Adam or Evangeline or whatever little cousin Evadne may have. Three, discussions on those subjects closed. SWALK" I kissed her.

"What does that mean?"

"It's what men in the forces put on the backs of envelopes when they write to their sweethearts. Means sealed with a loving kiss. I've just done that, so let's go to bed."

I was padding out to the bathroom to brush my teeth when I saw the cablegram envelope just inside the door. The cable had been sent from Cape Town. I read it twice before I fully understood it.

REGRET INFORM YOU MY FATHER DAVID GREENER DIED HEART ATTACK ON PLANE JOURNEY BACK HERE STOP HE WAS CHIEF WITNESS IN KLINE ROSS MURDER CASE STOP SORRY CANNOT HELP WITH YOUR FURTHER QUERIES RE IDENTIFICATION

PAULINE GREENER

I took it in to Rose, who was already in bed. "Look at this. Of all the luck."

"What is it, Dave? I'm asleep." She lifted her head from the pillow and looked at the message. "Cablegram. Poor Mr Greener, dying on the plane. Does it matter?"

"Oh Christ, skip it."

"Terribly sorry, darling, if it's bad news. Tell me in the morning…" Her voice trailed away, and she was asleep.

I didn't go to sleep so easily when I closed my eyes. The whole extraordinary day was mixed up in my head, and all the people in it were mixed up too, Crambo wearing Beverley's oily smile, Christy Freeman saying that we were all one big happy family, Rose swelling like a balloon until two little pink pigs popped out of her, squeaking "I'm Adam… I'm Evangeline" and she deflated with a sigh. When I opened my eyes I couldn't be sure whether I'd been dreaming or whether I'd really been half-awake all the time. Probably dreaming, because I had no idea what the time was. I looked at my watch, and it was a quarter to one. Rose was snoring. I lay with my eyes open staring into the dark, and remembered where it was I'd seen the man with straw-coloured hair who had been leaving the Follies Club. I had caught a glimpse of him in the Gongora Hotel, on the night I took Christy Freeman there. Just a glimpse through a half-open door, but I felt sure I was not mistaken. I spent some time in brooding on what his presence in the Follies Club meant, decided it probably meant nothing, and fell asleep.

Chapter Thirty-Eight

It's funny, the way in which after a whole lot of things happen that seem decisive, life goes on just as before. On Friday evening in the Follies Club it seemed to me that the conversations I was having with Beverley, Dimmock and Sir Henry were in some way final, and that I could never go back to my old relationship with Gross Enterprises. And Rose, too – surely we'd successfully come round a difficult corner in our marriage, and things would be different now? But on Saturday morning everything was the same as usual. Rose got up and cooked breakfast, slopping about in the dressing gown that had the top button missing, and saying she had a terrible head. My tongue was thick and furry and my eye had blackened up, although not as much as I expected. I put an eyeshade over it, which looked rather distinguished. The only thing changed was that when Rose said she didn't want any breakfast I made a clucking noise and told her to remember she was eating for two. She managed a smile at that.

The office also was as usual. My presence there on Saturday was accounted for by the fact that we worked a six and two, had done since before my time. There was no necessity for it really, but somebody – probably Jack Dimmock – must have calculated that working this way gave the staff the impression that the place was an inferno of industry and kept them always on the alert. It was a fact, too, that Saturday and Sunday always seemed to be days on which a lot of good ideas emerged. Or perhaps it was simply that Sir Henry had worked out that most people worked a five and two, and that this way he was getting quite a bit extra out of us over the whole year.

On my desk I found a note in Harold Paynter's copperplate hand. "Here is the story on the Star Chamber questioning of Sir Geoffrey Morgan. I flatter myself it has come out rather well." I played over the stuff and found that Paynter as usual was quite right about flattering himself. The story was just about as corny as could be, and I didn't see how we could use it. I tried to get hold of Paynter, but he was on his two days' leave. George Pacey came in, and I told him what I thought.

"Frankly to me Paynter's just a pain in the neck, and I don't know why he's here."

"He's an old-timer. Turned out some good stuff in the past, you know." I made a rude noise. "There's still more market than you'd think for this kind of ripe corn."

"If you say so, but I'm not having it in *Crime Magazine,* ripe or green."

"You're too hard on him, Harold has his uses. What's happened to the eye?"

"Officially conjunctivitis. Privately I had a fight with a swing door and the swing door won."

"How's the magazine coming?" I said all right, wondering as I said it whether it would ever appear under my editorship after last night. "Have you got time to run through a new story for me? I'm up to my neck with this changeover. It's one of Mary's in typescript, just needs a few frills putting on it."

"Be glad to. I'm not all that busy today." He put the typescript on my desk. "I was talking to Charles Peers last night and he told me there wasn't any election. Was that a joke."

George was on his way to the door. He turned round slowly. "What?"

"Election", I said patiently. "For the magazine editorship. Came to me through the death of the late lamented Willie, instead of on a vote as expected. Charles said there wasn't any vote. Did he mean what he said?"

George Pacey's face was a mask on which I could read nothing whatever. "I said before that the best thing you can do is to keep your nose out of all that. Let the police do it. That's all I can say, Dave, and it's good advice."

When he'd gone I settled down to read Mary Speed's story. It was called *Murder in Multum Parva,* and was sub-headed "A Nurse Grigson Story". We turned out three or four Nurse Grigson stories a year, and they were a very popular line. Nurse Grigson was a good solid middle-aged character who was always taking jobs where she had to look after a rich invalid old lady or gentleman who lived in some remote country house where there were no problems about servants or food. The old invalid was often murdered, and there was an assorted cast of relatives young and old as suspects. The old ones were generally amiable eccentrics and the young were engaged in love affairs that weren't running too smoothly.

Nurse Grigson was always falling in love with the young men in the stories, who were good Rugger-playing characters just down from the University, but she would gallantly stifle her feelings and clear up the misunderstandings that had caused the young women (generally kittenish cuddly types, but occasionally delicate dreamy creatures) to be distrustful of the young men, or vice versa. Incidentally or accidentally she would discover the murderer, who always turned out to be the local doctor or solicitor or some other professional figure. There would be quite a bit of village gossip, one or two garden parties or cocktail parties, a little flirtatious love-making, and lengthy descriptions of the women's dresses and of the food that everybody ate. The trick was to keep each story essentially the same so that readers knew exactly what to expect from Nurse Grigson, and yet to make the details different enough for them to feel they were getting value for their library subscription. Mary was good at it, and she wrote most of the Nurse Grigson stories, though other people had done them when she was busy – including Harold Paynter, who managed them reasonably well, being a kind of a middle-aged old woman himself.

Murder in Multum Parva proved a very fair specimen of its kind and I didn't find much to do to it. Crippled old Lady Anerley, who suffered from a heart complaint, was rash enough to venture down to the greenhouse in her wheelchair. There the key was turned on her and she died, not from suffocation but by some mysterious form of poisoning. Crawling out of her wheelchair in the way that old ladies do in mystery stories Lady Anerley had scrawled the name CLARE on the misty greenhouse window-pane. Since this was the name of her daughter, a kittenish little brunette given to curling up on sofas with a young stockbroker who was behaving rather oddly to her because he had foolishly got tangled up with a pretty nasty actress who was demanding marriage, the police naturally put Clare at the top of their suspects list. Nurse Grigson, however, disposed of the actress by discovering that she was married already, and traced the poison to a rare flower known as the "death orchid", the scent of which if inhaled for more than a couple of minutes was fatal to people suffering from Lady Anerley's particular heart trouble. And the name on the windowpane? Just a piece of would-be cleverness by the murderer, a solicitor named Maclaren, who had briskly wiped off three letters at the beginning and end of his name, thus leaving a pointer to Clare. The story ended with Nurse Grigson receiving an invitation to Clare's wedding.

As I've said it was a good average kind of story and didn't need many frills adding, just a bit of stockbrokery conversation from the young hero and an extra scene for the solicitor, who came through rather dimly. I recorded that without much trouble, and I cut out a bit of Nurse Grigson's homespun philosophy, on which Mary was inclined to spread herself a bit. Then I re-read part of the book and got on the line to Mary.

"Murder in Multum Parva", I said. "Very creditable, Nurse Grigson."

"Thanks, Dave. How's it going?"

"Well enough, except that I ran into a door last night." It occurred to me that if I was going to tell that to everybody I might as well take off the eyeshade, and I did so. "I've added and subtracted here and there, nothing to mention. Just one point I wanted a word about."

"I know, the death orchid. It's perfectly true, I got it from an orchid specialist. If you've got a maiden aunt with heart disease and plenty of money and she's left it to you and you can get her into a greenhouse and lock the door you'll be all right. As long as I get my ten per cent."

"Not the death orchid. The trick about Clare's name. Who suggested that?"

She sounded surprised. "Oh that, well it's just routine stuff, nothing special about it. Anything wrong?"

"Nothing wrong with it at all. Just wondered what put it in your mind?"

"I don't know, Dave. Nothing special. There was a story I did where we worked out the murderer's name through a crossword puzzle, and another one where it was in a kind of code. I daresay I had them at the back of my mind. If you want me to change it – "

"No, it's fine as it stands. I was just curious. Thanks, Mary."

I wrote down the names Clare and Maclaren on a pad and sat looking at them. Then I unlocked the drawer of my desk in which I kept the report on the Kline-Ross case and looked through it, searching to see if a certain name was there. It was, and I had a ridiculous idea that somehow didn't look so ridiculous the more I looked at it. For a little while I didn't know what to do with the idea. Then I remembered something Christy Freeman had said, I thought of the man with straw-coloured hair, and I knew what my next step should be.

Chapter Thirty-Nine

The Gongora Residential Hotel looked just the same. The windows were still uncleaned, the opalescent bowl outside was streaked with dirt. Inside there was the same smell of stale food. The hall was empty and I banged the bell that stood on the desk. I was in luck. The man with straw-coloured hair shot out from a door marked "Private". Now that I saw him this close I noticed that the something wrong about his eyes was a pronounced squint.

I didn't know quite how to start the conversation. "I want the manager."

"You're looking at him."

"Oh yes. You're Mr Papadopoulos."

"The name's Saunders, George Saunders. I'm a busy man." Above a puffy mouth which he tried to make tight was a short pathetic upper lip and the putty wedge of nose that I remembered. Above that again were the squinting blue eyes, somehow essentially innocent. A little man trying to keep up with a big rough world.

"I'm looking for a man named Morgan, who used to be here."

"He's gone. Done a moonlight flit."

"No address?"

"No address. Can't help you."

"Haven't we met before somewhere? In the Follies Club last night, for instance?"

"Not me. You must be thinking of two other people. I've got a lot to do." One eye swivelled wildly round the hall, embracing the dust, the grime, the threadbare carpet. The other stayed disconcertingly looking at me. Perhaps it was glass.

"It will keep, it's kept for a long time. You know who I am, don't you?"

"Don't know you from Adam."

"You ought to, because I saw you before last night at the Follies. On Monday evening. Just a glimpse through a door, but it was enough for me. I was with a woman named Christy Freeman."

He raised the short upper lip in a sneer. "And I don't know her from Eve."

"You're protesting too much, Papadopoulos, you're going too far. Because there's no doubt you knew Christy Freeman. And she's dead. That could happen to you too."

With upper lip drawn up, projecting teeth sticking out defiantly, he was a rabbit at bay. "My name's Saunders. And I know who you are now, you're Nelson. Inspector Crambo told me about you."

"Brilliant." Feeling very ridiculous, I advanced on him and took him by the shoulders. He backed against the wall. "Why don't you tell the police what you know, Saunders? What do you think you're going to get by keeping your mouth shut? Whatever it is, believe me it isn't worth it."

To my own astonishment I saw that these remarks had their effect. His teeth were almost chattering. "I don't know what you mean."

"You know what I mean but you haven't got the sense to act on it. I'm not sure how many years you get for being an accessory after the fact, but they put you away in prison for a long, long time."

I let go of him and stepped away. He was trembling, and his upper lip was working up and down. I believe there were actually tears in his eyes, or in one of them at any rate. His small hands were balled into fists. He stamped his foot. "Go away."

A woman poked her head out of a door at the end of a dark passage. "The butcher 'asn't been, Mr Saunders, what am I going to do for lunch?"

He said to me again, shrilly, "Go away."

"All right", said the woman indignantly. "If that's yer attitude I will." She closed the door with a bang.

"Now you've lost your cook", I told him. "Not that it was much loss, by the smell. I'll go away, I can tell when I'm not wanted. But it's good advice I've been giving you."

I left the hotel, walked smartly up the street and turned the corner. Here there was, conveniently placed, an ABC teashop. I went in by the side door, ordered milk and a dash and a Bath bun, and settled down where I could watch the entrance of the Gongora. I was betting that Saunders had been told not to use the telephone, and I was right. After about five minutes he came out, looked nervously up and down the street and then walked in my direction, looking for a taxi. I got up, paid my bill, and stood in the doorway out of sight. Two minutes after Saunders was in his taxi I was in mine, using words to the driver that I had never thought to hear outside one of our dictabooks: "Follow that taxi."

Saunders' taxi took him to a tall, narrow building in a Bloomsbury square. I told my driver to go past slowly, and as he did so I noted the number, twenty. We stopped and waited on the other side of the square. Saunders was in the house about ten minutes. He came out still looking worried, walked jerkily along the street and hailed another taxi. My guess was that he would be going back to the Gongora hotel after leaving a message, but I was not interested in George Saunders any more.

My driver was a little dark Jew with curly hair and a toothbrush moustache. I asked him to come with me, and together we walked up to the house where I pointed out to him one of the names on the door. Then I asked him to take me to the nearest telephone box, and there I rang up Rose. She answered the telephone immediately, but her voice was breathless as if she had been running.

"Dave, where are you? Have you seen him?"

"Seen who?"

"The Inspector, what's his name, Crambo? He wants to talk to you. I told him you were at the office, and he said you had been there but you'd gone out."

"In about ten minutes I shall be back. I'll talk to him then."

"Dave, I think he's – " She stopped, and started again. "He was so queer, awfully sharp and official, not the way he has been at all."

"Just showing his true colours I expect."

"Oh Dave, be serious. I think – could it be that – he's found some fresh evidence?"

I was aware, all at once, of things I'd temporarily forgotten: my aching eye, my lame foot, the narrowing circle Crambo had talked about, a circle of rope.

"Is there anything he could find?" Her voice was anxious. "Think, Dave."

I ran a hand over my forehead, gently touching the eye. "Rose, I've got no time to listen. I want to tell you – "

"But is there anything he could have found? If there is, I think he's found it. I think he's going to arrest you, Dave."

"I see." Now I remembered Crambo's words. *The rope is already hanging over his shoulders, but so lightly that he can't feel it. Every check we make on every minor point draws it just an inch tighter.* It was not a warm day, but I felt uncomfortably hot.

"Dave, are you there?"

"I'm here. You think he'll be waiting at the office, or have somebody there?"

"I'm sure he will."

"That makes what I've got to tell you more important. If they do arrest me, there are some things I want you to do." I told her what I'd found out, about Mary Speed's story and Charles Peers and this man Saunders and everything. She listened without interrupting. When I had finished she said, "But I can hardly believe it. Do you really think it can be true."

"I don't think, I'm certain. Now I've got to try to get proof. And if I'm unlucky and get pinched you'll have to find it, Rose."

"Yes."

"Promise?" She said she promised. "Believe in me? Wish me luck." She made a queer inarticulate noise. I hung up, went back to the taxi and told the driver to drop me in the street at the back of Gross Enterprises.

"Bad news?" He was sympathetic. "Dirty work, this kind of case."

"What kind?"

"Why divorce. That's what you're after, ain't it, and you want me as a witness. Knew it as soon as I looked at you. I'm your man, guv, I know all about it, believe me. I've had a basinful." He swung neatly from under the wheels of an advancing Bentley. "My first wife Norma, she left me for a travelling salesman. 'Course I hadn't got my own cab then, so you might say she had reason on her side. He left her flat in six months though, you never know where you are with birds like that. Turned into a sort of hostess at a little place down our way, and I used to pay to dance with her. Pay for a dance with your own wife now, you wouldn't credit that, would you?"

"But you married again?"

"Sure I did, and who did I marry? Some mothers do have 'em. Got myself hitched up with Norma's sister Vilma. Very like Norma she was, only not such a sweet nature. Came home one night, found she'd skipped with all my savings, gone off with some lad what promised to make a film star of her. Did all right for a year or two, Vilma did, till the slump came. Ended up on a beat in Piccadilly. Come to think of it, I paid her money too."

"Were there any more in the family?"

He nipped through a light just after it changed to red. "No, more's the pity. Lovely girls, both of 'em. Been married long?"

"Several years. And you're wrong, I'm not after divorce evidence. But you're right about wanting you as a witness."

"Any time, guv. Bennie Mendelssohn, 63 Pluckett Lane, just off the Commercial Road. Nothing I like more than a day in the Divorce Court, expenses paid."

"I told you I'm not after divorce evidence. Did you marry again?"

"Not me, guv. Had enough of it. Comes a time when a man's got to look after himself in this world, isn't that so?"

"I expect you're right."

"Here we are then. Whatever it is you're looking for I hope you find it. Don't forget the name, Bennie Mendelssohn." He gave me a great wink as I paid him off. I wasn't quite sure what he meant by it.

Chapter Forty

I reckoned that if Crambo was really intending to arrest me, he would have a man in the entrance hall of the offices, so that I shouldn't get more than ten yards inside the place before being picked up. I had remembered that the building next to ours, Proven Steel Products, was a companion office block to that which housed Gross Enterprises. The two blocks had been built at the same time and were only a few feet apart, a gap too far to jump but easily bridgeable by a ladder.

I happened to know that there was a ladder that might do the trick on the fourth floor of our building. It was kept in a cupboard, and I had seen the caretaker taking it upstairs to get out on to the roof. It occurred to me that there was probably a similar ladder in the Proven Steel building and that I might be able to get hold of it and use it as a bridge to get across to our roof. Perhaps this sounds unnecessarily romantic, but I took quite seriously what Rose had told me on the telephone. She obviously took it seriously herself.

I walked into the Proven Steel building and went up four flights of stairs without being questioned. I was in luck. On the fourth floor I found a twenty-foot extending ladder in two sections, in a cupboard exactly similar to that in Gross Enterprises. I blessed the uniformity of building planners, took out the ladder and carried it with some effort up to the next floor, where I easily found the trapdoor that led to the roof. I passed half a dozen people but none of them made the slightest attempt to stop me. There's nothing so convincing as a man apparently doing a tedious job of work. I placed the ladder against the trap door and climbed up it.

Out on the roof I pulled the ladder up after me. The next step wasn't so easy. I had somehow thought of the roof as flat, but in fact this part of it sloped gradually down to a chimney, and the gap to the similar chimney on the Gross Enterprises building looked uncommonly wide. I scrambled down the roof until I was behind the chimney stack, pulling the ladder down after me. At one point I turned over my lame foot, and thought I should faint with the pain of it.

The pain ebbed away, and it occurred to me that I should have been wise to buy some rope. But I had no rope, and I could see no way of getting the ladder across except by fixing it on to the chimney pots on either side. I stood up with the ladder, lifted it over the gap – and nearly toppled down the hundred odd feet to the street through underestimating the ladder's weight and its outward pull. It took four attempts before I got it fixed to my satisfaction, that is, as far as you can fix anything satisfactorily which can be tested only at the risk of your life. I held on to the chimney stack and put my weight cautiously on the ladder. It seemed fine. I began to crawl across it.

I cannot describe the crossing of that swaying ladder, with nothing between myself and death but a narrow piece of wood precariously lodged on two chimneys. I don't suppose it took me more than sixty seconds to crawl across, but when it was over and I was on the roof of our building my heart was thudding so much, and my hands were so unsteady, that I had to rest. Those were sixty seconds of pure terror, and if I had had any idea of what they would be like, I should have walked into the hall of Gross Enterprises and chanced the coppers.

After the crossing the rest was comparatively easy. I hauled the ladder over after me, clambered up to our skylight, lowered the ladder inside it and climbed down on to our fifth floor. Everything was just as I remembered it, the lighting concealed discreetly, the corridor thickly carpeted. On the left was the lift, and on the right the door that led to Dimmock's black and green office. At the end of the corridor was a door marked "Private". I took a chance, opened it, and found myself looking straight at Sir Henry Gross.

This was his office. It was much more comfortable and less grand than Jack Dimmock's. There was a big desk littered with papers, a row of telephones and a two-way dictograph for listening and talking. There was a Turkey carpet on the floor, a large sofa and a couple of matching armchairs, all slightly shabby. Sporting prints lined the walls and there was an overdressed cocktail cabinet in a corner. It was what you might call a homey sort of office. At the moment Sir Henry was not attending to business. He was asleep with his feet up on the sofa, breathing quietly. He looked very grey and tired.

I walked across to the dictograph and put up the switch. There was one of these machines in every executive's office, so that anyone who put down their own switch would hear us talking. Then I stood in front of Sir Henry and coughed apologetically. He opened his eyes. They were watery grey, bleary and small, an old man's eyes, and at first they did not seem to see me. Then he struggled to a sitting position and fiddled with his collar, which was undone.

"Why, Nelson, how did you get in here?"

"I wanted to talk to you."

"But you talked to me last night." He said it as though that ought to be my ration for a few weeks.

"I'd like to speak to Mr Dimmock too. What's his extension?"

"This is very extraordinary behaviour." His hands were trembling, he couldn't get the stud through the collar and he left it. "His extension is number one", he said weakly.

I dialled *one* and when I got an answer said: "Sir Henry would like to speak to you. Right away." I put down the telephone.

Sir Henry pulled at his lean grey jaw in an agitated way. "This really is an unwarrantable intrusion, Nelson. Things like this cannot go on. I cannot recall a similar – um – invasion of my private office for several years."

It was the longest speech I had ever heard him make. I made no answer to it.

Somebody said: "Sir Henry, Dave. Thought I recognised the voice." Jack Dimmock stood by my side, hands spoiling the jacket pockets of a beautifully cut tweed suit. He looked perfectly composed, which was more than I was myself. I had been expecting him to enter by the door I had used, but instead he had come through another that was set in the wall. Silly to be upset by a little thing like that, but it put me right out of my stride. Dimmock reached out a hand to brush me down. "You're dusty."

"Yes." I began to brush roof and ladder dust away from my clothes in a desultory way.

"If it's about last night, that's forgotten."

"It's not about last night. I know who killed Willie Strayte."

"You do?" Dimmock's tone blended surprise, congratulation and a hint of amusement. He looked more Napoleonic than usual, the Emperor about to tweak the ear of a promising young General. "High time, Dave, if I may say so. I didn't tell Sir Henry, but Inspector Crambo came up to see me half an hour ago. He's very keen to have a talk with you, Dave." Now the amusement was predominant. It was very well done, perhaps a little too well done. It had the effect of annoying me and settling me down again.

"I think you ought to hear about it."

"You do, Dave? Got anything in the way of proof? Perhaps you ought to talk to Crambo straightaway." Now there could be no doubt of the mockery in his voice.

I had been concentrating on Dimmock so completely that I had almost forgotten Sir Henry. It came as quite a surprise to hear him croak, "Let him talk."

Dimmock nodded. "All right, Dave, let's have it. Might be a story here for the organization. Make it fast, though. I've got a conference in half an hour. Who killed Willie Strayte?"

I took a deep breath. "You did."

Dimmock laughed. "Perhaps I ought to give Crambo a ring and ask him to come up now. Can't think how you missed him on the way."

"Let him talk", said Sir Henry.

"That's right, let me talk, hear what I've got to say. Half an 'hour can't make any difference here or there, can it?" I strolled over and sat in the swivelling armchair at the desk, by the dictograph.

Dimmock watched me with his thick brows together in a puzzled frown. His voice when he said, "Let's have it then", was innocent of anything but a businesslike crispness.

"I won't begin at the beginning, that goes too far back. I'll begin at the point where Willie Strayte met a man named Greener, a few weeks ago. The meeting was a matter of pure chance, some friends of Willie's in South Africa had given Greener an introduction. Willie asked Greener to call for him one day at these offices and here, probably in the entrance hall, Greener saw a man he knew. Greener had been chief witness in a murder case years ago. It took place in South Africa and was known as the Kline-Ross case. In it two half-brothers named George and Alec Ross received sentences of death and twenty years' imprisonment. They escaped a few days after the sentence. Greener saw and recognised one of these brothers. He saw George Ross."

Sir Henry sat on the sofa, grey-faced and collarless, his hands wrapped one over another. Jack Dimmock said: "And in this speculative piece of yours, who did Greener recognise as George Ross? Me? I should think I'm a bit young for the part.".

"Not you." I said to Sir Henry, "Your name is Henry George Ross. When you came over to England you simply called yourself Henry Gross, adding the first letter of your Christian name to your surname. Criminals often feel a compulsion to keep something near to their own names, instead of changing them completely. I was looking for your young half-brother Alec – I'd quite forgotten about Henry George until this morning. Then I read a detective story that had a similar clue in it and I realised that Henry Gross was very much like Henry G Ross."

Dimmock didn't sound admiring or amused or businesslike now, just plain angry. "You'll be able to produce this man Greener, of course."

"No. Greener was a sick man. He had a heart attack and died on the plane journey back to South Africa, as I expect you know. But there must still be other people alive who could identify Sir Henry Gross as Henry George Ross. Now that we know what to look for we shall find them."

Dimmock rubbed his chin. "Allowing that your wild story has any truth in it, I doubt if that's so. It's a long time ago, and unless you're lucky you'd have to do a lot of searching. Frankly, Dave, I don't think you'll have time to search. I think Crambo's got *you* tagged for it."

"What happened to Alec?" I asked Sir Henry. "I suppose he's dead? I was foolish to think only of Alec and to forget Henry George."

"If that's all, Dave, I'll get hold of Crambo", said Dimmock.

"It isn't all. You'd better hear everything I've got to say, so that you know all the answers." I looked at the switch of the dictograph, pushed up, and prayed that somebody was listening.

At that Dimmock frowned again. He couldn't understand what I was getting at, and I didn't blame him. "All right. Make it quick."

"As quick as I can. There's no indication that Greener meant to do anything about seeing Ross, but in the stress of the moment he said something to Willie Strayte. Whatever he said was enough to send Willie snooping in our files, where as luck would have it he found a report on the Kline-Ross case. Don't interrupt. I know Willie could have been looking up material for a story, but in that case where did the file get to? Taking the file was a mistake."

"Willie primed himself with the story and then asked to see one of you, probably Sir Henry. He asked for the editorship of *Crime Magazine* as the price of keeping silent, and he got it. Accordingly, an innocent character named Dave Nelson who had expected to get the editorship was disappointed, and tried to work out which of the section Editors had cheated on him in voting. Nelson was mistaken. There wasn't any voting, just an instruction from above that Strayte was to be appointed editor. If Nelson had had a brain in his head he'd have guessed that long ago, from what he was told. Any observations?"

It was Sir Henry I wanted to get at, but Dimmock was the spokesman every time. I didn't like that. He was too tough to break. "Hard words, Dave, but we thought Strayte was the better man. More brains, as you've hinted."

He looked with raised eyebrows at Sir Henry. "Quite so", the old man said. "Quite so."

I said to Dimmock, "What about that tale you spun me about the election being democratic, and your surprise when Hep told you the editor was to be Willie Strayte?"

Dimmock met my gaze candidly. "Don't recall that conversation. Afraid you've invented it."

"But Willie was greedy. For him the editorship was only a first step. He must have made that plain when he asked you to come round and see him." I swung round to Sir Henry. "Did he take you along?"

"No, no. I didn't know anything about it until – "

"Shut up", Dimmock said. Sir Henry stopped.

"It was Dimmock on his own then, as I thought. Whatever Willie asked for, it was too much. There was a quarrel and he was killed. I'm willing to believe it was unpremeditated, but it was murder just the same. That evening Dave Nelson, the perfect stooge, was drowning his sorrows by picking up a tart named Christy Freeman. When I told Christy who I worked for she said something about it being a small world. I thought she meant she knew somebody at Gross Enterprises, and so she did, but she meant a bit more than that. You didn't give up all your gang contacts, Jack, when you packed it in with the Barcini brothers, and took to being a shark in the City. You run the Gongora Hotel through a nominee, don't you? Half a dozen others too, very likely."

"Don't call me Jack. You're crazy."

"Oh no I'm not. I had a chat with George Saunders, the man you put in there. He got frightened and ran round to your flat to leave a message. I've got a taxi-driver witness to that. Saunders isn't reliable, Jack, believe me. I should get rid of him if I were you. Is that what happened to Morgan, or did you give him the money to hide out somewhere?"

Dimmock stared hard at me, his nostrils wide. Then he smiled, and the smile was charming. "All right, Dave. Have a drink on it and tell me what you want. Whisky?" He went over to the cocktail cabinet and poured three large whiskies. They all came out of the same bottle and the soda was squirted out of the same syphon for all of us.

Sir Henry took his hesitantly. "I never touch spirits."

"Drink it." Dimmock treated me now as though we were partners and had a common opponent in Sir Henry. "Cheers, Dave. Now, what do you want?"

"Chiefly I want to go on talking. Because now I'm coming to the scene which you can't play for anything but the biggest laugh ever heard on any stage. You know the one I mean. The scene in which Dave Nelson, knowing he's a suspect, goes to see Jack Dimmock and solemnly tells him the whole story of his actions on the night of the murder. The meeting with Christy, the visit to the Gongora Hotel, the whole thing delivered on a plate to the man who really knew how to make use of it. What a laugh you must have had, Jack, behind that stare of yours."

"It was funny." Dimmock rested that same stare on me now, not at all as though he thought it funny.

"It was funny. You promoted me to the editorship, neatly underlining my motive for police purposes. Then you must have acted fast. First you had to tell the boys at the Gongora to be like Brer Rabbit and say nothing. Don't want to get the hotel in bad with the police, that would have been the line. Whatever they ask you the answer is no. People like Morgan and Saunders don't like talking to the police anyway and they wouldn't make any trouble. But then there was Christy Freeman. You couldn't just tell Christy to keep quiet, you had to see to it yourself."

Dimmock lit a cigarette and drew on it. "I don't see what you want, Dave. Is it some kind of a deal?"

"What about – " I jerked my thumb at Sir Henry.

"Oh, him." The tone was contemptuous. "Let's have your proposition."

"Just let me finish. Correct me where I'm wrong. You let Christy have it on Tuesday, after talking to me. That very fact, the time when she was killed, should have told me who did it. Because I had the advantage of Crambo in knowing I hadn't killed Christy, though sometimes I felt so crazy I thought I might have done it. But if I was innocent who could have done it on Tuesday, who knew that I wanted her as a witness? There was only one person, the man I told before I told the police – my big-hearted uncle Jack Dimmock."

"You were slow on the uptake", Dimmock agreed. "You were always slow on the uptake about some things, Dave."

"My uncle. Father confessor. Just to make quite sure there shouldn't be any doubt who did it you burgled my flat, left Christy's address there, took a few things out of it and parked them in the room where she died. I suppose the way it was meant to work out was that the police would find Christy, come to my flat and discover her address. It misfired a bit because my wife got hold of the paper with the address on it, and we did a little investigating. I found the cigarette lighter you'd planted, but nothing else. I suppose there *was* something else, and Crambo's got hold of it."

"A gin bottle", Dimmock said calmly. "Must have had your prints all over it."

Sir Henry made a whistling noise in his throat and got up from the sofa. I had almost forgotten him. "I knew nothing of that. You must believe me, Nelson, he told me nothing of that. I should not have permitted it."

"I admire your ethics, Sir Henry. You think it was all right to knock off Christy Freeman, but Jack shouldn't have left that trail of clues to me."

"No, no, young man, you mistake me. I am an honourable man."

Dimmock stood up too, stocky and formidable. He threw away the cigarette and put his hands in his jacket pockets again. "You old fool, shut up. I'm tired of all this gab. Can we fix it on him, Dave, is that your proposition?"

I ran my hand over my forehead. It was wet. I could not feel any pain in my eye, it was as though it had been anaesthetised. I could feel perspiration soaking my armpits and my thighs. I looked imploringly at the dictograph switch and then at the door. Had anything of what we were saying been overheard, or was it all wasted effort?

"A couple more words to get the record straight about Beverley. Then I'll come to the proposition. Of course you realised that even if you planted the crime on me it would do a lot of harm to Gross Enterprises. No doubt you'd rather have found your suspect outside the firm, but as it was you had no choice. With Venturesome creeping up on sales you'd probably been considering making an arrangement with Beverley for some time. This made it urgent, and no doubt you'd decided to sell out before he began to get hold of your executives by offering fancy prices. You were being smart with him at the time he thought he was being smart with you. I thought that scene of gloom last night at the Follies Club was too good to be true."

Sir Henry moved slowly towards the door that led into the corridor.

"Where are you going?" Dimmock repeated it when the old man went on. "Henry, where are you going?"

"I've had enough, too much. I'm going to talk to the Inspector."

Dimmock put his hand to his hip and brought out a revolver, stubby and blue. I looked at the thing in absolute fascination. I must have written or revised a hundred scenes of this sort and now that I was involved in one the only impression I had was of its theatrical unreality.

"Henry." Dimmock's voice was pleading. "I shall use this if I have to. Don't make me use it, Henry."

Crambo's voice, close by me, said "Don't use it, Dimmock. It's no use, we've got a record of almost the whole thing. Just stay where you are, all three of you." I never thought I should be glad to hear Crambo's voice.

Dimmock stared at the dictograph, as if thrown out in an intricate mathematical calculation by some mistake like an error in simple addition. He said to Sir Henry, "You bloody fool." I recall that his tone of voice was not at all angry, rather regretful.

Then he fired the gun, shooting first at Sir Henry and then at me. There seemed to be so many bangs that I could not count the shots. They made a tremendous noise. I was not conscious of any fear at all, and I remember thinking: "Absurd, the whole thing's a comic opera, he's firing blanks."

With something like a sense of awe I saw Sir Henry sag slowly to the ground with a hand pressed to his side. "Oh", he said, and repeated in a low, moaning voice: "Oh, oh, oh."

Dimmock darted away through the door in the wall, and from behind it I heard another bang, to which I paid no notice at the time. I went over to Sir Henry and tried to shift him on to the sofa. "Are you hurt?" I asked. "Did he hit you?" He made no reply, but simply kept groaning, "Oh, oh."

Then the door from the corridor opened and the room was full of people. Crambo I recognised, and one or two of the men who had been at Christy Freeman's flat. George Pacey, Hep,

Mary Speed, some others. "Where is he?" Crambo asked me. I pointed to the door in the wall and then heard myself begin to giggle foolishly.

Mary said, "Dave, your arm. You've been shot."

I went on giggling. "Don't be silly, Mary. That must be old Sir Henry."

"Dave, it's *dripping.*"

I looked down at my left arm and it was quite true, the coat sleeve was wet and blood was dripping from it. This seemed to me so funny that my giggle turned into a laugh. The room swayed up and down in front of me, and I found it impossible to stop laughing.

Chapter Forty-One

I woke up with somebody holding my hand. I moved my eyes around and looked down at the hand that held mine. It was narrow, with pink-tipped nails. Turning my neck carefully, rather as though it might break, I saw that Rose was sitting on the sofa by my side. The sofa was the one in Sir Henry's office.

"Rose."

"Hallo there. How do you feel?"

"Fine." I looked at my left arm, which was bandaged. "What happened to that?"

"Nothing very much, a flesh wound. The doctor takes it lightly, says it was nervous strain more than the wound that made you faint. We'll go home in a minute."

"How did you get here? What's the time?"

"Half past three." I had been out for more than an hour. "The Inspector telephoned me."

"Glad he had that much decency. Didn't know he was a friend of mine."

She said lightly, "You're bit of a hero, you know, Dave. Solving a crime single-handed, getting wounded and all that. You've got lots of friends suddenly. They're queuing up to come and see you."

She went to the door and they all trooped in, my pals. George Pacey and Bill Rogers and Hep and Mary Speed and Sol Birkett and even Miss Richards. They all came in to see the wounded warrior, they asked how it felt to solve a real murder mystery. I hope I made the right answers.

Bill Rogers said with some embarrassment, "I owe you an apology, Dave, about last night. Flew off the handle. You know what it is, sometimes just a little thing does it."

"Forget it."

"But I really am sorry, I want you to know that. Sonia was wild at me." I could see what he meant. It was like hitting a man and then finding out he'd won the VC.

"Skip it. I've forgotten all about last night. *All* about it", I said with emphasis.

His battered red face, with the air of experience on it that had been gained in many bars and bedrooms, went a shade redder. "Thanks, pal."

My pals. They were all good chaps, as good as they had ever been, but I seemed to see them differently. They were as nice as any other people, but I found I just couldn't believe a word they were saying. I knew there wasn't one of them who hadn't believed at some time or another that I'd killed Willie Strayte.

When they had gone Crambo came in through the door in the wall, with his insurance salesman's smirk. "How's the conquering hero?"

"As well as can be expected. You left things a bit late."

"I wanted to hear the whole story, and I didn't think he had a revolver, or if he had one that he'd use it. I was wrong." Like everybody else he sounded apologetic. "Lucky for you he was a bad shot, so bad he even made a mess of shooting himself. Pointed the gun upwards and the bullet went through his shoulder. He'll stand trial." Crambo's laugh was hearty but false.

"Sir Henry?"

"Sir Henry's dead. Dimmock used four bullets on him and they didn't all miss."

"Were you going to arrest me?" I asked Crambo. He didn't answer. "What was the new evidence you'd found?"

"Your fingerprints all over a gin bottle in Christy Freeman's flat, as Dimmock said. I wanted to talk to you about it."

I raised myself on the sofa and spoke angrily. "Why don't you admit you were wrong all along the line, Crambo?"

"I was waiting for something or someone to break."

"You were waiting for the moment when you could put your hand on my shoulder."

He shook his head. His voice was brisk but mild. "If I'd believed in the case against you I should have had you under lock and key long ago. You didn't help by withholding the details of your interview with Dimmock when you were appointed editor. But there's no point in talking about it now. You're overwrought, and I'm not surprised. You'd better go home." His voice softened as he spoke to Rose. "Good luck to you both."

Rose said nothing as we were taken home in a police car. Back in the flat she sat me down in my own armchair and brought me a large whisky. I drank it and felt more like a man. The rubber band had gone from my forehead, my eye didn't ache, the arm scarcely bothered me.

"The conquering hero", I said. "A couple of days ago they were all looking forward to seeing me in the dock. They make me sick."

"Dave, do you love me?"

"How many more times do I have to say yes to that?"

"And you're fed up with being on the merry-go-round, you really want to step off it?"

"Fed up to the back teeth."

"Then what about that caravan? You can make enough to live on as a freelance. I'm not worried about nylons, Dave, honestly, my legs are good enough without them. Why don't we do it, Dave, why don't we?"

"Why not? I can't think of any reason."

"Then it's settled." She came and sat on the floor beside my chair and I stroked her hair. It was fine, silky hair. I told myself that we were both the right side of forty, not too late for making a new start. I told myself I was happy.

Chapter Forty-Two

That should have been the end of the story, but it wasn't. The door bell rang. I stopped stroking Rose's hair. She didn't move. The bell rang again.

"Don't answer it", she said. "Let it ring."

"Better go. Maybe Crambo's changed his mind about arresting me."

"Don't answer it", she whispered.

I got up and went to the door. I daresay I knew before I opened it that Beverley would be standing there. He shook my hand, waddled in, bent over to Rose and kissed her on the cheek. "Aren't you proud of him, my dear?"

She said without looking up: "Yes."

"When I heard what he'd done there were tears in my eyes. I cried like a little child, and that's the truth. You faced that murderous villain with his gun, Davy boy, you grappled with him barehanded – "

"That's not quite right. I just stood there."

He waved a fat ringed hand. "You stood there without flinching, and defied him to do his worst. And the way you got him to talk, and admit just what had happened. You've got a head on your shoulders, Davy boy. This is a great story, the story of the century, and we're going to tell it that way."

"Tell it that way", I echoed stupidly. Rose didn't move.

"Those scoundrels", Beverley said unctuously. "Those wicked men. When I think how nearly I was trapped into partnership with them I shudder. I owe you a debt of gratitude, Davy boy, and I'm going to pay it. Gross Enterprises is finished, you realise that."

I hadn't thought about it. "Yes, I suppose it is."

"One principal of the firm dead and the other on a murder charge. Well!" Beverley laughed happily and then became serious again. "I'm going to see that none of the boys I talked to lose by it. Venturesome is going to expand and all of you executives are coming on the pay roll. And you especially, Davy, I want you as my personal assistant."

"Personal assistant."

"We'll run your story as a special opening issue of our own crime magazine. The whole issue given over to Dave Nelson's struggle with gangsterdom in his own organization. Think what it means to you, Davy boy."

"Think what it means to you", I said.

Beverley laughed and laughed. "You're all there. Your husband's all there, isn't he, my dear?"

"I hope so", said Rose.

"He's a lucky man, and especially lucky to have such a charming wife. I often ask myself, what good does all the money in the world do you without the love of a good woman? And do you know what I answer? I say, Jake, when you find a good woman what will you do with the half-dozen bad ones you've got in tow? It's settled then, Davy, and here's my hand on it."

Rose said, "Dave."

"I don't know", I said to Beverley. "I just don't know. Anyway the story is worth more than five hundred now."

"Five hundred, seven fifty, a thousand, if there's one thing I never haggle over it's money. And that goes for salary too. You leave it to Jake, and you won't be the loser."

"I haven't been the winner yet." He laughed again, he could find humour in anything, that man. "I don't know, I'll have to think it over."

Rose got up and went into the bedroom.

"You do that." He patted my good arm avuncularly.

"And then you ring me up on Monday and if you're the smart boy I think you are, Davy, I know what answer you'll give me. We're going to be in the money at Venturesome, and I want to see that you get your cut."

After he had gone down to his Rolls I went into the bedroom. Rose was putting on a cream facial mask and her face, one side white and the other still flesh-coloured, stared at me from the glass.

"I didn't promise anything, I said I'd let him know. You heard that."

She said nothing, but continued to spread the cream.

"We'll talk it over together, you and I. Don't think I was letting him sell me a line, Rose. It just might be worth putting off the caravan for six months, that's all, if there really is money in it."

I could read no expression on Rose's face and she said nothing, but I knew what she was thinking and I knew she was right. I knew that I'd go in with Beverley and there would be no caravan for me, now or in six months or ever. I knew that somehow I couldn't do anything else. I remembered what Charles Peers had said about the circular theory of personality, and what he'd said seemed to make an awful lot of sense at this moment. *I am repressed, therefore I am... Our actions move within a narrowing circle of possibility, we are like goldfish swimming in an ever-contracting bowl.*

Now Rose's whole face was white as a clown's. From this dead mask her living eyes, in the glass, looked sorrowfully out at me.

Julian Symons

The Broken Penny

An Eastern-bloc country, shaped like a broken penny, was being torn apart by warring resistance movements. Only one man could unite the hostile factions – Professor Jacob Arbitzer. Arbitzer, smuggled into the country by Charles Garden during the Second World War, has risen to become president, only to have to be smuggled out again when the communists gained control. Under pressure from the British Government who want him reinstated, Arbitzer agreed to return on one condition – that Charles Garden again escort him. *The Broken Penny* is a thrilling spy adventure brilliantly recreating the chilling conditions of the Cold War.

'Thrills, horrors, tears and irony' – *The Times Literary Supplement*

'The most exciting, astonishing and believable spy thriller to appear in years' – *The New York Times*

Julian Symons

The Colour of Murder

John Wilkins was a gentle, mild-mannered man who lived a simple, predictable life. So when he met a beautiful, irresistible girl his world was turned upside down. Looking at his wife, and thinking of the girl, everything turned red before his eyes – the colour of murder. Later, his mind a blank, his only defence was that he loved his wife far too much to hurt her…

'A book to delight every puzzle-suspense enthusiast'
– *The New York Times*

The End of Solomon Grundy

When a girl turns up dead in a Mayfair Mews, the police want to write it off as just another murdered prostitute, but Superintendent Manners isn't quite so sure. He is convinced that the key to the crime lies in The Dell – an affluent suburban housing estate. And in The Dell lives Solomon Grundy. Could he have killed the girl: so Superintendent Manners thinks.

Julian Symons

A Man Called Jones

The office party was in full swing so no one heard the shot – fired at close range through the back of Lionel Hargreaves, elder son of the founder of Hargreaves Advertising Agency. The killer left only one clue – a pair of yellow gloves – but it looked almost as if he had wanted them to be found. As Inspector Bland sets out to solve the murder, he encounters a deadly trail of deception, suspense – and two more bodies.

The Players and the Game

'Count Dracula meets Bonnie Parker. What will they do together? The vampire you'd hate to love, sinister and debonair, sinks those eye teeth into Bonnie's succulent throat.'

Is this the beginning of a sadistic relationship or simply an extract from a psychopath's diary? Either way it marks the beginning of a dangerous game that is destined to end in chilling terror and bloody murder.

'Unusual, ingenious and fascinating as a poisonous snake'
– *Sunday Telegraph*

Julian Symons

The Plot Against Roger Rider

Roger Rider and Geoffrey Paradine had known each other since childhood. Roger was the intelligent, good-looking, successful one and Geoffrey was the one everyone else picked on. When years of suppressed anger, jealousy and frustration finally surfaced, Geoffrey took his revenge by sleeping with Roger's beautiful wife. Was this price enough for all those miserable years of put downs? When Roger turned up dead the police certainly didn't think so.

'[Symons] is in diabolical top form' – *Washington Post*

TITLES BY JULIAN SYMONS AVAILABLE DIRECT FROM HOUSE OF STRATUS

Quantity		£	$(US)	$(CAN)	€
	The Players and the Game	6.99	12.95	19.95	13.50
	The Plot Against Roger Rider	6.99	12.95	19.95	13.50
	The Progress of a Crime	6.99	12.95	19.95	13.50
	A Three-Pipe Problem	6.99	12.95	19.95	13.50
	History/Criticism				
	Buller's Campaign	8.99	13.95	20.95	15.00
	The Tell-Tale Heart: The Life and Works of Edgar Allen Poe	8.99	13.95	20.95	15.00
	England's Pride	8.99	13.95	20.95	15.00
	The General Strike	8.99	13.95	20.95	15.00
	Horatio Bottomley	8.99	13.95	20.95	15.00
	The Thirties	8.99	13.95	20.95	15.00
	Thomas Carlyle	8.99	13.95	20.95	15.00

ALL HOUSE OF STRATUS BOOKS ARE AVAILABLE FROM GOOD BOOKSHOPS OR DIRECT FROM THE PUBLISHER:

Tel: **Order Line**
0800 169 1780 (UK)
1 800 724 1100 (USA)
International
+44 (0) 1845 527700 (UK)
+01 845 463 1100 (USA)

Fax: **+44 (0) 1845 527711 (UK)**
+01 845 463 0018 (USA)
(please quote author, title and credit card details.)

Send to:

House of Stratus Sales Department
Thirsk Industrial Park
York Road, Thirsk
North Yorkshire, YO7 3BX
UK

House of Stratus Inc.
2 Neptune Road
Poughkeepsie
NY 12601
USA

PAYMENT

Please tick currency you wish to use:

☐ £ (Sterling) ☐ $ (US) ☐ $ (CAN) ☐ € (Euros)

Allow for shipping costs charged per order plus an amount per book as set out in the tables below:

CURRENCY/DESTINATION

	£(Sterling)	$(US)	$(CAN)	€(Euros)
Cost per order				
UK	1.50	2.25	3.50	2.50
Europe	3.00	4.50	6.75	5.00
North America	3.00	3.50	5.25	5.00
Rest of World	3.00	4.50	6.75	5.00
Additional cost per book				
UK	0.50	0.75	1.15	0.85
Europe	1.00	1.50	2.25	1.70
North America	1.00	1.00	1.50	1.70
Rest of World	1.50	2.25	3.50	3.00

PLEASE SEND CHEQUE OR INTERNATIONAL MONEY ORDER
payable to: HOUSE OF STRATUS LTD or HOUSE OF STRATUS INC. or card payment as indicated

STERLING EXAMPLE

Cost of book(s): .... Example: 3 x books at £6.99 each: £20.97

Cost of order: .... Example: £1.50 (Delivery to UK address)

Additional cost per book: .... Example: 3 x £0.50: £1.50

Order total including shipping: .... Example: £23.97

VISA, MASTERCARD, SWITCH, AMEX:

☐☐☐☐☐☐☐☐☐☐☐☐☐☐☐☐☐☐☐☐

Issue number (Switch only):

☐☐☐

Start Date: ☐☐/☐☐

Expiry Date: ☐☐/☐☐

Signature: ____________________

NAME: ____________________

ADDRESS: ____________________

COUNTRY: ____________________

ZIP/POSTCODE: ____________________

Please allow 28 days for delivery. Despatch normally within 48 hours.

Prices subject to change without notice.
Please tick box if you do not wish to receive any additional information. ☐